About the author

R J Turner is a Shropshire lad, born and brought up in
Bridgnorth. He attended Goldsmiths' College studying
speech and drama. While there he wrote a prize-winning
one-act play and had some poems read on radio. Later
he obtained a degree at Bristol University.

Family commitments meant that he had to
concentrate on teaching and he eventually became a
headteacher. Since retirement he has returned to
writing, including a full-length play, a short story read
on radio and several prize-winning poems. Two
contemporary crime novels, set in Shropshire, have

been published by Leaf by Leaf Press: *A Perfect Alibi* and *Murder On The Moss*.

He has returned to Shropshire with his family but loves to visit and be visited by his daughters, grandson, granddaughters and great granddaughters. He also has a son, still living at home. He is fascinated by local history and loves to walk his dog in the local countryside around Oswestry, where he now lives.

WICKED HARVEST

R J Turner

WICKED HARVEST

Vanguard Press

A CIP catalogue record for this title is
available from the British Library.

ISBN 978-1-80016-496-3

*Vanguard Press is an imprint of
Pegasus Elliot Mackenzie Publishers Ltd.*
www.pegasuspublishers.com

First Published in 2022

**Vanguard Press
Sheraton House Castle Park
Cambridge England**

Printed & Bound in Great Britain

Dedication

To my long-suffering wife, Madeline. An author's wife is a difficult life.

Acknowledgements

My thanks go to Derek Williams, former librarian at Oswestry Library and secretary of the Oswestry and Borders Historical and Archaeological Group, who first read the text for its historical accuracy and made many useful suggestions. Thanks also to the Oswestry Writing Group for listening to many chapters of my novel with patience and for their constant help and support.

A special thanks to Kirstie Edwards for her very professional assistance as copy editor and proof reader and incidentally for her painting, which is used in the cover design.

My thanks go to Pegasus for accepting my novel and to the production team for their prompt attention to my many questions.

I would also like to thank my son Robert for his assistance with proofreading.

Oh! My God the down,
The soft young down of her, the brown,
The brown of her — her eyes, her hair, her hair!'

'The Farmer's Bride' by Charlotte Mew 1878–1917

ONE
South Shropshire 1879

John Noble, the new master of Hope Underhill National School, closed his books, stood up and stretched out his arms. He had moved into the schoolhouse just three days ago and spent most of the time since preparing for the term ahead. Now, he was ready for a good walk in the afternoon sun, a rarity this year. His housekeeper, Mrs Bywater, had told him they were cutting the last field of barley today, up near Squire's Copse, so he would take his walk in that direction.

There was no one about on this warm late August afternoon. Even the village shop was closed. The only sign of life was an old brown dog, which struggled to its feet as John passed, wearily wagged its tail a couple of times, then sank back into the dust.

John took the Churchtown road, which climbed steeply out of the village and after half a mile or so he turned left into Manor Lane. Soon he reached the copse and went through an open gate into a field.

Copse Field was an *okkard bogger*, as the locals would say; small and steeply sloping, halfway up Long Hill, just below a stand of trees that separated the cultivated fields from the wild moorland above. Much of the barley had been flattened by storms in June and July, but the last few days of fine weather had ripened the bent stalks and given a chance to get in some sort of harvest.

All that remained of this year's crop was a rectangle of barley about twenty yards wide and twice as long, in the centre of the stubble field. John joined the other villagers who had come to see these last few swathes gathered in. Some of the older men and women remembered him as Farmer Noble's son and tugged their forelocks or gave a slight curtsey in recognition. Together, they watched the driver lead the horses forward and heard the clickety-clack of the old reaping machine and the hiss of the wooden paddles, as they pushed the stalks towards the scissoring blades which laid them low.

One man balanced on a little platform at the back of the machine and raked off the stalks for the other harvesters to gather in their arms and tie into sheaves. These sheaves were leaned against one another in stooks, ready to be loaded onto the wagons and taken back to the farmyard for threshing.

The dozen or so workers employed to harvest the crop were almost lost among the crowd of onlookers in the last field. Women and children shuffled forward in the stubble where the barley had been lifted, to glean for grain that had been missed by the machine or shaken from the sheaves and fill their pockets to feed the chickens back home. Boys, thankful to be out of school for the harvest month, stood poised in the stubble, watching the wall of barley just in front of the machine, ready to pounce on the rabbits which would shoot out in panic and race for the safety of the hedgerow. It took just one skilful dive and a hand clasped round the animal's legs as it jerked and squirmed, then a sharp blow to the back of the head, and one family at least would have a decent meal that night.

These were hard times. The newspapers were calling it the "Great Agricultural Depression", with summers so bad that most of the crops were lost and any grain garnered was thin and sour. Even when the crops were gathered the price was so low, because of all the cheap grain coming from abroad, that farmers had no money to buy stock or fertiliser.

If they had been frugal in the good times and sufficient funds remained, many tenant farmers had given up and gone to the towns for work or retired. But it was the ordinary working folk, as usual, who suffered most. Wages fell as low as nine shillings a week, where work was to be got; where not, the workhouses were full.

'Christ almighty!'

John's reverie was shattered by a terrible cry. The reaping machine had halted and the driver was vomiting violently next to the hedgerow. People began to move towards the machine, but Gabriel the rake man leapt down and stopped them. His ruddy, weathered face had turned white as chalk. For some reason, he came to John.

'Mr Noble, you must come and see!' Then he turned to the others. 'Go home, the lot on you. There'll be no more harvesting today.'

Gabriel had once worked for John's father as an apprentice dairyman. He was a big man with a commanding presence, so the workers did as they were told. John followed him towards the reaping machine. Gabriel unhitched the horses and shooed them away, then he pointed towards the blades of the machine. John advanced slowly and a smell came to him. He had come across it in Africa, several times. It was the smell of decaying flesh.

John edged carefully around the machine and saw a heap of blue fabric caught in its blades. As he moved closer, he could see it was a dress, and a black cloud of flies was swarming over the remains of a woman's face, although it was impossible to distinguish any features. The remains of a hand and wrist emerged from one sleeve but scavenging creatures had already begun their feast.

John felt vomit rising in his throat. He gasped as he was reminded of his long dead wife, but this was not Elizabeth. Her body lay under a baobab tree beside a lake in the middle of Africa.

He was not sure why Gabriel had chosen him to take charge. Perhaps he knew that John had lived in Africa and may have seen horrors not normally witnessed in the English countryside. Or perhaps, to Gabriel, he was still the boss's son. Either way, John knew what had to be done. He was certain that the woman had been dead for several days at least, but that formalities had to be observed.

'Gabriel, go and fetch the doctor and the rector. I'll cross the hill and notify the constable. And don't move the body or anything around it till the constable has been.'

Gabriel nodded and strode away towards the village. John set off in the opposite direction, up the western slope of Long Hill towards Churchtown, which lay three miles away in the next valley.

As he began to climb, the sun weakened and thick clouds gathered behind him over Devil's Peak. He would be lucky if he reached Churchtown before heavy rain began to fall.

TWO

As John began to climb to the top of the Long Hill he saw again, in his mind's eye, the wicked sight of that corpse in the blue dress. He wondered who the woman was and how she came to be lying dead in a field of barley?

It was nine years since John had last seen a harvest, in Hope Underhill, but that was the hay harvest on his father's farm. At twenty-one he'd just come down from Cambridge where he'd struggled through his finals, because there were so many better things to do than sit in his room, mugging up on Greek or wading through dull tomes on divinity. He much preferred to go rambling through the Cambridgeshire countryside with his friend Paul.

It was on one of those rambles that he had met Elizabeth out walking with a friend. At that first meeting the couples chatted briefly about the weather and where their walks were taking them, but John managed to work out that the girls lived in a village a few miles north of the city and that they must be home in time for the service at the chapel that evening. It would have been far too obvious to pretend a sudden conversion to Methodism and follow the girls to that service, so the boys planned an excursion much closer to their village for the following Sunday, and just happened to be passing the chapel when the evening service began.

Afterwards, they were asked to join the other worshippers for refreshments and the four young people were naturally drawn into conversation again. Elizabeth was quite plain, but her rather severe features were softened by light brown hair and hazel eyes. Her figure was full and might soon become plump, but she glowed with youth and health, and her conversation was intelligent.

Elizabeth's father, Thomas Smithson, was the schoolmaster at the British School in the village, a nonconformist foundation. At first, Mr Smithson was slightly in awe of the younger man, owing to his privileged background and university education, but they shared an interest in natural history and soon they were firm friends, which meant John no longer had to use subterfuge to spend time with Elizabeth. Their relationship developed so naturally that Mr and Mrs Smithson were quite agreeable when he asked if Elizabeth could spend part of the summer with him and his parents at Hope Underhill, hoping that a more formal relationship might follow.

Elizabeth loved everything about John's home. The landscape with its steep hills and deep valleys astonished her after the perpetual flatness of Cambridgeshire. She was delighted by the farm and took great interest in all its activities. She had no fear of the animals and didn't care if her clothes got a little spoiled. She was soon a favourite with the labourers and trusted to help with collecting eggs or bringing the cows in for milking. She became close to Mrs Noble and the two women were often heard giggling together down the garden path.

The only stumbling block was Mr Noble. A staunch conservative by upbringing and inclination, Mr Noble thought of nonconformists as agitators against everything he held dear and thought, at first, that Elizabeth would not make a suitable wife for his son. But when his son made it clear that he was to become a missionary, in Africa, his father began to see that Elizabeth's health and strength along with her sensible, practical approach to life, would be excellent qualities for a missionary's wife.

Before Elizabeth's return to Cambridgeshire, John wrote to the Smithson's asking permission to marry their daughter. There was a prompt reply agreeing that when he had completed his training with the Missionary Society, he could marry Elizabeth and she would go with him to Africa.

Sometimes, when they were alone, the couple shared a shy embrace and John would press his body closer, but Elizabeth would quickly pull herself free, fanning her pink cheeks with the little Bible that she always carried and turning rapidly to examine some aspect of the landscape which she asked her companion to explain.

When Elizabeth returned to Cambridgeshire John felt an emptiness in his life, so he threw himself into the hay harvest. He joined the other workers in the fields, following the skilled men with their scythes — his father would have no new-fangled machinery on his farm — and using his pitchfork to make haycocks from the stiffening brown grasses. The hay would be turned every few days until it was dry enough to be collected together and built into stacks.

As John lifted and tossed the hay he kept noticing one of the women working beside him. She was different from the others, darker skinned, with long black hair tumbling down from its pins to rest on her bare neck. She wore the same long skirt and cotton blouse as the other women but somehow her clothes revealed more of her female form and she had a way of moving that drew attention to her fine figure. She was not popular with the other women. They called her a foreigner and made disparaging remarks about her morals because she came from the other side of the Welsh border, but she did not seem to care. She was always smiling at something a man had said or flashing a belligerent glance at some woman's comment before giving a barbed reply. John could not help glancing at her and from time to time she looked back at him, holding his stare and smiling enigmatically.

When he first came to the field in the morning John would look for her, and if she was there, he would settle quickly and happily to his work. On the odd occasion that she was absent, 'Sleeping it off,' or 'Giving her arse a rest,' as one woman said, he found the work wearisome.

One evening, after a particularly warm day, when he had drunk too much cider to soothe the tickle of dry dust in his throat, John sought the shade and privacy of a small wood to relieve himself. As he was rebuttoning his breeches he was shocked to see the woman emerge from a nearby bush, giving a momentary glimpse of her white flesh before shaking out her skirts. He found himself quite unable to move, until she turned towards him. He looked away quickly but she did not seem in the least discomfited. Instead, she walked towards him, smiling.

'What's the matter, my love? Ain't you seen a woman's arse afore?' She came a little closer, and her smile widened, as she added, 'We all 'as the same needs you know.'

'I... I...' John stammered.

Instead of turning and walking away, to cover her embarrassment, she approached him and looked him right in the eye.

'I seen you,' she began, in her sing song border tongue, 'watching me. Likes what you see, don't you, my love?'

Now that they were so close, John could see the woman was a little older than he had thought, thirty perhaps, or even more, with faint lines beginning to fan out from her large dark eyes, but her face was beautifully shaped, and when her lips parted, her teeth gleamed in the gloom of the wood.

'I'm sorry, I should not have...' but the woman simply laughed, put her arms around him and drew him close, making his heart beat wildly as he felt her firm bosom pressing against his.

'Never say you shouldn't. My youth is almost gone, I knows that, and it feels good to have a handsome young man like yourself looking at me in that way.'

Whether it was the heat of the evening or the hypnotic effect of those dark eyes John would never be sure, but instead of pulling away, he put his arms around her, pulled her closer and felt the warmth of her thighs pressing against him. Her hands moved down his back until her fingers pressed into his buttocks and his penis hardened. He began to moan softly, as he explored her. He felt as if he was floating, lost in a cloud of sensation, no longer able to control himself. Suddenly, the woman pulled away, took his hand like a child and led him back into the field, which was empty now. She pushed him back onto a haycock, unbuttoned his breeches, lifted her skirts and guided his stiffened member inside her. It was not long before he shuddered and felt an ecstasy flowing through his whole body. The woman sighed and lay beside him, equally content for the moment, then she brought a flagon of cider from the bottom of the haycock where it had remained cool. While they shared the sour sweet liquid, she told him that her name was Gwyneth, that she came from a village twenty miles

21

beyond the Welsh border and that she had been widowed for several years.

When the pleasure of his orgasm began to wane, John began to feel guilty, but when Gwyneth took hold of his member and brought it back to life, he lifted her skirts and plunged in again. This time their intercourse lasted longer, and she showed him how to increase her pleasure, so that his release, when it came, was more rewarding for them both.

Soon, the remaining warmth of the evening, the potency of the cider and the additional physical exercise after a long day in the field began to take effect, and he lay back on the hay and closed his eyes.

When he woke up, Gwyneth had gone. The night had turned cool and the stars shimmered against the deep black sky. Feelings of guilt at what he had done made him shiver violently. He rose stiffly from the flattened hay and made his way back to the farmhouse, tears stinging his eyes.

The next day John left the farm, telling his parents he needed time to think and pray before beginning his missionary training. He went into the wilderness of Snowdonia and walked, occasionally in sunshine but more often through chilling mist or wind driven rain. The worse the weather the more he walked, as if punishing himself. He knew that he could not go back to the farm until the season was over and Gwyneth had left. He wondered if he could ever face Elizabeth again.

THREE
South Shropshire 1879

John was alone on the road that wound its way across the top of Long Hill. Bracken and heather stretched for miles on either side with only clumps of gorse or the occasional wind-crippled tree interrupting the landscape. As he strode forward, sheep rose indignantly from the roadside and trotted off stiffly, bleating their irritation, and in the distance a group of wild ponies momentarily lifted their heads to watch him pass.

On a fine day this was beautiful place to walk or ride, but now that a grey wall of cloud in the west had obscured the sun and a chill wind began to hiss across the grasses, its character changed. Long Hill stretched north to south for a dozen miles, but when the light failed and the horizon was blurred, the moorland could seem bleak and endless. It was much easier then to believe the old stories about this place: of ancient massacres; of children carried off by supernatural beings; of spells cast on unfortunate travellers who disturbed witches at their rituals. John did not believe these stories, but he turned up the collar of his thin coat and hurried on.

To erase the image of the dead woman from his mind, John thought back to earlier, happier days during his time at Cambridge. The sun seemed to shine more often then as he wandered through the Fens, studying the flora and fauna and learning about the history of that flat, seemingly endless landscape.

Since his arrival at university, his interest in religion had steadily faded to be replaced by an obsession with geography and natural history. His friend Paul had introduced him to Darwin's *Origin of Species* which he had read in a few hectic sittings, both horrified and fascinated by the questions it raised about man's place on Earth.

Similarly, he had devoured the journals of Doctor Livingstone, who was at that time lost somewhere on the dark continent. John had no doubt that when his studies were over, he would follow the great man to Africa, but it was the thrill of exploration which inspired him, rather than the conversion of the heathen.

The cloud had caught up with John and a light drizzle began to fall. He increased his pace in the hope of reaching Churchtown before it became a downpour.

Finally, the road, which was cut into the hillside and was barely wide enough for a cart, especially where the edges had crumbled away, began to descend. He saw the little town below him, and what looked like a toy train puffing its way out of the station, heading north towards Shrewsbury.

He increased his pace as the rain grew heavier, and at the bottom of the hill he hurried towards the constable's office where he would report the death in the barley field. As the image of that mutilated corpse returned, he thought back to the first dead person he had seen.

FOUR
East London 1872

John had just begun his training with the Missionary Society and was working in London's East End. For the first few days he had been almost incapable of doing anything, so shocked was he by the conditions he found there.

At first, he toured the ugly, filthy streets and stinking alleys with a more experienced member of the mission staff. They visited the sick in hovels that heaved with human life; families of nine or more sharing a single room. He heard the story of a family who shared their room with pigs, so the floor was covered in manure and each child, in turn, succumbed to dysentery. He saw families living on the streets or trundling their few belongings in dilapidated handcarts along the cobbles, in search of cheaper accommodation in darker, more decrepit slums.

The shock faded into numbing familiarity and was then replaced by anger. This was England, one of the richest nations on Earth, with an ever-expanding empire across the globe. This was London, where Parliament met to pass laws ending slavery, reducing the hours to be worked by children in the factories and making sure with Forster's Act of 1870 that all children could attend school. This was the city where great exhibitions were held, visited by people from all over the world. Just a few miles west, the rich lived in splendid crescents and the middle classes enjoyed considerable comfort in the suburbs, from where they deplored the indolence and immorality of the poor.

Very few of these people ever visited the East End, and those who did were usually in search of excitement and entertainment because a sexual partner — man, woman or child — could easily be purchased for a few shillings.

With anger came frustration; John felt he had so little to offer. What was the point of his trying to turn these people into Christians? For most of them paradise would have been one good meal a day and a warm, safe place to sleep at night. How could they be afraid of eternal damnation when they were already living in Hell? All John could offer was some thin soup, inadequate medical attention and a story or two from the Bible.

After a few weeks, he was sent off on his own to visit a family who lived in the damp basement of a lodging house off the Mile End Road. The father was a dock worker, but he was a drunkard who never got to the docks early enough to be selected for work. The mother was getting thinner by the day, because whatever she could find to eat was given to her five children, and whatever she earned from washing clothes was stolen by her husband to spend on drink. The woman said she was thirty-five, but she looked like an old woman with her greying hair, sunken cheeks and loose skin hanging from her skeletal limbs.

John waited till the evening, when he knew that the husband would be out in search of alcohol. This was when the children got what sleep they could before their father came home to beat their mother and abuse them. John brought bread and a little cheese, so that they could, at least, have a few mouthfuls of food while he told them some of the Gospel stories. He chose those involving children, and as he spoke the familiar words from Matthew's gospel, "Suffer little children to come unto me", he watched the mother sharing out the food like a bird feeding her chicks. He tried to make sure that she kept some for herself but she told him she wasn't hungry. She smiled as the children settled back to sleep on the single bed, boys at one end and girls at the other, with their stomachs no longer gnawing, but the little party was interrupted by the father who had managed to get drunk earlier than usual and needed somewhere to lay his spinning head.

When he found John sitting with his family, he cursed him and accused him of seducing his wife. Then he removed his thick leather belt and wound it round his wrist to strike her. He aimed a blow at her head, caught her with the buckle and she dropped to the floor. The man was large and muscular, but out of condition and fuddled with drink. John felled him with a single angry blow and fled back to the mission.

Next morning John was told that someone was waiting to see him. It was the oldest of the children, a boy aged about eight. He looked up at John with red rimmed eyes and muttered brokenly, 'Please, mister. You gotta come. He's gone. Told us we was bastards and could manage without him. Said Mam were a whore.'

He followed the boy back to their lodgings, where the children were huddled against one wall, while their mother lay motionless on the opposite side of the room. He lifted the thin blanket from her face and knew at once that she was dead.

He arranged for the mother to be buried and paid for it out of his meagre allowance. He supposed that the children must go to the workhouse, but then someone told him about a remarkable man named Doctor Barnardo, who had opened a place for homeless children in Stepney Causeway, and who promised never to turn away a child in need. He took the little family along and they were admitted.

John became wracked with guilt and feelings of inadequacy. He could not eat or sleep properly and became so ill that he had to be removed to the mission's headquarters in the Essex countryside. It was from there that Elizabeth and her father came to take him back to

Cambridgeshire and nursed him back to health.

Later that year, John and Elizabeth were married, and the following February they set sail for Africa.

FIVE
Africa 1873 to 1875

On a cold, grey February morning their ship left Tilbury, disappeared into the Thames fog and began the long journey down the Channel and across the Bay of Biscay. The only boat that either of them had ever been on before was a punt along the Backs at Cambridge, so they spent the early part of the voyage being sick, while the wind and waves seemed always about to smash the masts, rip the sails, overturn their puny vessel and fling them to the bottom of the sea. At last, the skies cleared and the sun grew warm, then hot, as they followed the west coast of Africa down to the Cape of Good Hope.

When they reached Cape Town, they stayed, for a while, at the Missionary Society's headquarters. Here they met black Africans for the first time and were disappointed by the way the white people treated them; the natives were all servants of one kind or another, taken from their homes, apparently converted to Christianity and stripped of their heritage and dignity. John vowed he would never do the same. He remembered the admiration and respect that Doctor Livingstone had shown towards these people in his journals.

The young couple were given final instructions, maps, letters of introduction and supplies before embarking for Zanzibar, an island off the east coast of Africa, from where they were to begin their travels into the interior.

As the gateway to Central Africa, Zanzibar was crowded and crude; dozens of different nationalities thrust together by greed as they waited to exploit the enormous potential of Africa that lay cloaked in fog just twenty miles away. The port stank of sewage, wood smoke, cooking and animals, both dead and alive.

They had landed in April just as the monsoon season began and with it a cholera epidemic. Luckily, they were staying on another part of the island, some distance from the port, with an elderly couple who had retired from missionary service and were about to return to England. Both couples would have to wait until the monsoon was over before travelling, and it was while they were waiting, with increasing impatience, that news came through of the death of Livingstone.

John found their stay with the Bellingham's increasingly irksome. They were a pious, conventional couple, from East Grinstead, who had come out to Africa several years ago, but had never ventured further than Zanzibar. They viewed the Africans on the mainland as unredeemable savages and thought that he and Elizabeth were wasting their time, and possibly their lives, by venturing into the interior.

Elizabeth had discovered that she was pregnant and was quite happy to rest and gently assist Mrs Bellingham with her mission duties. John spent more and more time out of the house, exploring the island and particularly the port, where he was fascinated by the frenetic business of loading and unloading cargo from and for every part of the world.

One day he was directed to a far corner of the harbour, where he was told that an unusual cargo was about to arrive. The old man smiled strangely and warned him to keep out of sight of those on board the vessel. John was naturally curious and made his way to the very edge of the harbour, beyond the last buildings of the town. A jetty had been built right up against the jungle and was almost hidden by overhanging vegetation, making it very easy for him to see what was happening, without himself being seen.

A large Arab dhow was moored at the end of the jetty, leaving enough space on the landward side for a small vessel to tie up behind it. The crew of the dhow was busily preparing to sail but strangely there did not seem to be any cargo in the hold. John noticed that a young Arab boy sat astride the lookout post, high above the deck, even though the vessel was safe in the harbour. He was keenly scanning the horizon out on the Zanzibar Channel. Suddenly, the boy put up his hand to shade his eyes, then called something in Arabic to the crew below.

John stared out over the water in the same direction and saw the dot of a boat making for the harbour. As the vessel came closer, he could see that it was one of the ferry boats that constantly plied their trade between the island and the mainland. When it entered the harbour, he saw that the boat was low in the water as if heavily loaded and soon it was close enough for him to see that its listing hull was in fact packed with black bodies. The boat slipped sluggishly past the dhow and tied up behind it. Immediately several men from the Arab boat came towards it with rifles in their hands and greeted a couple of European men who had leapt from the boat as soon as it bumped against the jetty.

John watched in horror as a line of tall black Africans, yoked about the necks and chained together, were pushed and prodded onto the jetty, then marched shuffling and stumbling across to the dhow, where they were forced into its bowels. Then came women and children, mostly naked, linked with lighter chains. None of these unfortunate beings made a sound; the long journey and the fiery whips had already subdued them. Then, as the dhow left the jetty and crossed the harbour, probably heading for some place in Arabia, as John had been told, a sound rose from the vessel; a sad lament as the slaves bid farewell to their homeland.

John had thought slavery long abolished — the whole western world condemned it — yet he had seen it for himself. He returned to the Bellingham's' house full of anger and told them what he had seen.

Bellingham told him that, of course, the slave trade continued, but that was Arab business, not theirs, and one could not interfere with a completely different culture. He informed John that the treatment of slaves was much improved these days, and that Africans would be far better off living as servants in a civilised Middle Eastern country, than rotting in godless ignorance in some filthy jungle village.

Next day, a message came from the British Consul that a boat had been found to take them across the channel whenever they were ready to go. Mrs Bellingham was disgusted that John was prepared to take his wife on such an arduous and dangerous journey in her condition, but Elizabeth was happy to leave. These were the early days of her pregnancy and it would be much better to get to their destination and then have her baby, than to take a newborn infant on the journey. So, the very next day they bade Mrs Bellingham farewell — Mr Bellingham was nowhere to be found — and boarded the vessel that was to take them across to the mainland.

SIX
Africa 1873 to 1875

The journey was long and difficult, involving a steamship up the Rovuma River, a trek by mule across the highlands, a crossing by canoe of a crocodile infested river, and finally a long haul along the shore of a large lake.

When they reached the abandoned mission, the few bearers who had remained loyal helped them to patch up the house and the little church beside the lake. As soon as they were able to move into the house, Elizabeth went into labour, but the journey had been too arduous and the baby was stillborn. Over the next two years Elizabeth suffered several miscarriages and John decided that it was safer and kinder not to continue a marital relationship, seeking physical satisfaction with a series of local girls, who succumbed to his status in the community and his tall European stature.

After the last of these infidelities, he returned to the mission full of guilt, but Elizabeth was too tired by her miscarriages to care. They were much happier together without John's frustrations simmering away between them. For a while, he gave all his attention to his wife and they both tried to make a success of their marriage and their mission, but without children and with very few converts, both were ill-fated.

Eventually John accepted that they must leave Africa, although they had not yet completed their three-year contract with the Missionary Society. His reading of Darwin at Cambridge had weakened his faith; their failure as parents and missionaries had ended his belief. He knew that it would be very hard to convince Elizabeth, but as it turned out no persuasion was necessary. Elizabeth became very ill, and without medical aid of any kind, a few months later she was dead. John buried his wife under a baobab tree beside the lake, closed the mission, and began the long journey back to the coast.

It was the lowest point of his life. He had failed as a missionary, failed as a husband and even failed as an honest man because he had never told Elizabeth about his infidelities. He needed God more than ever, but no longer had any faith to sustain him.

When he got back to Zanzibar there was more bad news. A letter from his father was waiting for him. His mother had died several weeks earlier, during an epidemic of scarlet fever that had spread through the Long Valley. His father had written at once but his letter had never reached the mission.

On the long, lonely voyage back to England, via the recently opened Suez Canal, John leaned on the rail, watching the ocean skimming by, and thought how easy it would be to fall into the green depths and end it all.

But he knew that such an act would kill his father and that Elizabeth's parents needed him to comfort them over the death of their daughter. He had no plans for when he returned to England and no hopes at all for the future.

SEVEN
South Shropshire 1876

It was midwinter when John made the journey back to Hope Underhill and the landscape matched his mood, with its leafless trees, damp meadows and dreary skies. Farming was beginning to decline and his father's farm looked neglected. He appeared to have aged far more than the three years it had been since John had seen him last. He showed little interest in his son's return and no real sympathy for the collapse of John's hopes or Elizabeth's death. He simply sat, murmuring, ''Tis all gone, all gone.'

Then one morning his mood changed.

'We'll go and see 'er this morning. I anna seen her in a while.'

It was the first time John had seen his father shaved and properly dressed since his return. As they walked to the churchyard, it was as if they were going to see a living being, rather than a mound of earth and when they reached the grave, his father's face lifted again, and he seemed to be gazing at his beloved wife, as he murmured, 'Don't worry, Sarah. I wunna be long.'

On the way home, he told his son that he would be giving up the farm next quarter day and going to live with his sister Alice in Shrewsbury. John was glad; he could not have coped with responsibility for his father at present. He made sure that one of the farm worker's wives would look in each day until his father moved to Shrewsbury, paid her a generous advance, and left for Cambridgeshire to visit Elizabeth's parents.

The Smithson's could not have been more different. They were mourning, but they wanted to know all about the life their daughter and her husband had shared in Africa, how she had died and where she was buried. For their sakes, John put a positive filter on their African adventure, stressing the kindness of the natives, the success of the mission and the beauty of the country. He mentioned nothing of those lost children or of Elizabeth's terrible suffering at the end. And by sharing his memories with them in this way, his own gloom began to lift. He admired the bravery of the Smithson's in coping with the loss of their daughter, and he realised this was partly because they had other children to be concerned about. Elizabeth had been the eldest of three daughters, and Mr Smithson had a school to run while his wife busied herself with their home and the many charitable activities with which she was involved.

At last John began to consider his own future. The Missionary Society had allowed him to keep the remainder of his stipend, but that was dwindling fast. He had explained that he did not want to continue as a missionary, which they understood, and without actually revealing the fact that he had lost his faith, he made it clear that he had no inclination to take on a parish, even as a curate. But he still had to earn a living, so what was he to do? It was during his stay at the Smithson's that the answer came.

One day, he visited the little school to watch his father-in-law in action. At first the older man was a little disconcerted, but then he asked John if he would assist a couple of the older pupils who were struggling with their arithmetic. Within minutes John was lost in the task and was delighted when one of the boys he was helping looked up, smiling, and said, 'I see, sir. Yes, I get it now.' For John, too, it was a moment of revelation. He moved around the class, helping other children with their work and was astonished when Mr Smithson announced that the school day was over.

On their way home, his father-in-law said simply, 'Well, my boy, I don't need to ask what you are going to do. We must find you a place at a teacher training college as soon as possible. Yes?'

John grasped his father-in-law's hand and shook it firmly, saying, 'Yes. Oh, yes!'

He entered a training college the following autumn and then became a teacher, at first in a newly opened Board School in Bedford, where he worked under a tyrannical head teacher, appropriately named Payne, but after a couple of years he began to look for a smaller school in the country, where he could develop his own way of teaching. Just as things were settling down and he was beginning to develop a new life, Aunt Alice sent news from Shrewsbury that his father was very ill and that she was too old and frail herself to cope with her bedridden brother. John resigned in late May and when the term ended in July, he reluctantly made his way to Shrewsbury. He was only just in time; his father died a few days later.

Aunt Alice explained that her brother wanted to be buried in Hope Underhill next to his beloved wife, so arrangements were made and John found himself returning to the place of his birth behind a horse-drawn hearse.

After the ceremony, he got into conversation with the rector, a tall, thin gloomy bachelor in his late forties, who had arrived in Hope Underhill a couple of years before and seemed quite unhappy with the place and its people.

'No respect for education. No respect for the true religion. Just want to mumble the old hymns and let the church decay. They think that attending a service, excuses their sinning for the rest of the week. And sin is rife!'

Here was an unhappy man, thought John, but when he explained that he was searching for a teaching post, the rector's face lit up.

'That is quite remarkable. A wonderful example of God's mysterious ways. Just a few days ago, I received a letter from the mistress of the village school, where I am correspondent for the managers, explaining that she, quite unexpectedly and immediately, had to leave the village and could not continue in her post. With the new term so close, I had little chance of finding a suitable replacement and then you arrive, for the sad purpose of your father's funeral, but nevertheless, as the ideal candidate for the vacant position. The Lord be praised! Please tell me that you will take the post. The managers will easily be persuaded in the circumstances. And you may move into the schoolhouse as soon as you wish. Promise me here and now that you will become the master of our village school?'

John asked for a little time to consider the matter. He explained to Aunt Alice, before she set off back to Shrewsbury, what had happened and saw the relief in her face that she would not have to take on another lodger. John walked through the village, and then took the Churchtown road, up onto Long Hill. He wanted to stretch his legs after the journey from Shrewsbury and the hard pews of the parish church. It would give him time to consider the Reverend Whiting's offer but he knew already that he would accept.

The managers of Hope Underhill National School were happy to take the rector's advice and offer John the master's post. He was suitably qualified and had some experience, and of course they all remembered his father. So, John moved into the schoolhouse and began to plan for the new term.

It was as a break from such planning that he had taken a stroll up the hillside and stopped to watch the

43

barley being harvested. Now, here he was, approaching Churchtown to seek out the constable and give him the disturbing news of the corpse in the barley field.

EIGHT
South Shropshire 1879

Constable Oakes was young. He was round and ruddy in the face with a bush of blond hair that would not sit down properly on his large head. A decade ago, he would have been a farm labourer, but now the farms had more than enough labourers and a constable's pay was slightly better and more regular. When John brought him the news of the corpse in the barley field he became flustered and the ruddiness spread and deepened.

'A woman you say? Dead like? In a barley field?'

'Yes.'

'Well now, and whereabouts is this 'ere barley field?'

'Copse Farm. That's the first farm after Long Hill going down towards Hope. Just below the trees.'

'Ah, I knows it. An' you reckon she be proper dead?'

'For some time, I would say.'

There was a considerable pause after each question while Constable Oakes licked his lips and wrote laboriously in his notebook in a large round hand.

'And who be you that's telling me this?'

'My name's Noble. John Noble. I'm just appointed master of the school in Hope.'

'No, you bain't. They got a mistress. And right pretty she be.'

'She had to leave, suddenly. I'm taking her place.'

The look on the constable's face while he chewed his pencil suggested that his thoughts were dwelling on the 'right pretty' mistress of Hope Underhill School rather than the body in the barley, but he suddenly straightened up as if he had remembered his official role and a worried frown crossed his youthful brow.

'I anna 'ad a corpse to deal with afore. Reckon I'll telegraph the office in Shoosbry. Then you must take me to the place where this 'ere body were found.'

So, when Oakes had telegraphed Shrewsbury, they set off in a dog cart borrowed from the nearest hostelry, a large new building on the crossroads, where the cart usually carried customers and their luggage to and from the railway station. Oakes lent John a spare constabulary cape, for the rain was now coming down in sheets. By the time they had crossed the hill it had grown quite dark and at first, John had some difficulty in locating the field. Then he saw the abandoned reaping machine standing like some strange dark beast with a tail of uncut barley behind it. It was not just his increasing hunger and the chill of the evening that made him shudder as they crossed the stubble.

Constable Oakes raised his lantern over the rain drenched body and retched. Then he put a hand over his nose and held the lantern closer.

'She be too far gone to say who she might be, but someone might recognise that dress. You say you sent someone for the rector and the doctor. Well, then we better be finding them and seeing what they 'ave to tell us. I told Shoosbry I'd meet their men at the Swan. They keeps a fine ale down there. And I can drop you off at the schoolhouse on the way.'

As Oakes walked away, the clouds parted and the moonlight revealed something which had not been noticeable in the day. In the contrast between moonlight and shadow, a path could be seen going through the barley and leading to the corpse. It looked as though the victim, or someone else, or both had trampled through the crop. John was about to point this out to Oakes when the clouds closed again and almost total darkness returned.

John was glad to have the constable's lantern to follow as they made their way back to the waiting horse and cart. When they reached the village, they found the Reverend Whiting and Doctor McKenzie standing in the church porch, sheltering from the resumed downpour. John thought that the rector looked quite ill as he hurried to join him, followed at a slower pace by Constable Oakes. Whiting let them into the church and lit a candle. Then he turned to John.

'This is a terrible business. I knew at once who she was. Not so much by her face, because that was terribly mutilated, but her dress, which she often wore in school. Poor Har... Miss Owen. Whatever can have happened?'

Doctor McKenzie was wheezing and muttering as he usually did before he spoke, like a bagpipe filling with wind, but the words finally emerged, in his strong Scots accent.

'She's been awhile deed, I can tell ye, maybe a week or more. But how she came to be deed I canna tell wi' the rain and all. She must be moved quickly to a cool place and examined properly by the pathologist.'

'I've telegraphed the office in Shrewsbury,' Oakes informed them. 'They're probably on their way right now. But it may be too late to take her up there tonight. We might have to keep her in the crypt, like. That being a cool and private place.'

'Oh, God!' the rector burst out, more as an expression of his personal anguish than a plea for his maker's assistance. 'No, that's impossible. I cannot allow it.'

Suddenly Oakes straightened his back and gave his voice a new tone of authority. Perhaps he would make a good constable after all.

'Now look, I ain't saying as that will 'ave to happen, but if it does, 'tis your duty to assist the police in whatever way you can. Now, I wants you gentlemen,' he said, indicating the rector and the doctor, 'to come along with me to the Swan and meet with whoever

48

Shoosbry sends, and pass on any information you can about this nasty business. And you, John Noble, may go back to the schoolhouse and take something to eat and rest yourself, for you surely have had a tiring evening. And if my superiors wish to speak to you later, I'll let you know.'

John was exhausted and his stomach gnawed with hunger. He bid them all farewell and went next door to the schoolhouse. The place was cold and damp, as if the rain had washed away the summer and brought autumn in early, but he hadn't the energy to make a fire. He simply lit the lamp, took a quick supper of bread, cheese and ale, and made his way to bed.

In spite of weariness, sleep was slow to come. Images of the day whirled round in his head. He kept seeing that swollen face and neck, covered with flies, lying there among the barley stalks, and the faded blue of that dress caught in the reaper's blades. Now he knew that those were the remains of a woman called Miss Owen, who until a short while ago had occupied this house, slept in this room, and whose decomposing corpse might already be lying in the crypt of St Mary Magdalene, just a few yards away.

It was not just horror that kept John's mind busy, but also a growing curiosity. He saw again the way the body had lain as if the woman had fallen head first but the force of meeting the earth had twisted round her head and neck. He remembered the moonlit path through the last swathe of barley. And as he pictured the path through the barley, he imagined a dark figure hurrying away.

NINE
South Shropshire 1879

The sun was well up when John was woken next morning by the sound of a door below him squeaking open and a woman's voice calling up the stairs.

'Mr Noble, are you there? Such terrible news!'

'I'll be down in a moment, Mrs Bywater.'

It was his daily help who lived with her husband, Sam, the verger of St Mary Magdalene, in a cottage just two doors away. She had looked after Miss Owen just as she was now looking after him. He dressed quickly and went down to find Mrs Bywater dithering about in the living room. Normally, she was a sensible woman who could cope with any difficulty life sent, but today she was wringing her hands, then lifting her apron to dab at her reddened eyes. It was John who had to be calm and sensible this morning, as Mrs Bywater set off again, pacing about and muttering.

'The poor child. 'Tis all she was!'

'Sit down, my dear. Calm yourself. I think I know your news already. I have a small bottle of brandy, kept for times like these.'

He poured some of the spirit into a glass and handed it to Mrs Bywater who drank it straight down without appearing to notice.

''Tis terrible! Terrible! That such a thing could happen here in Hope! 'Tis a wicked world we're living in!'

Then the brandy seemed to reach the right place. Mrs Bywater calmed down, wiped her eyes and looked at John as if she had just taken in what he had said.

'You know, then? About dear Miss Owen?'

'Yes, I was there when she was discovered. But how did you find out?'

'Oh, it were terrible. Sam, my husband, went into the church early, to fetch his spade from the crypt and there was this policeman standing by the door, telling him to keep away. Then they got chatting and the constable told him about the body. Next this other policeman, one of them as doesn't wear a uniform, comes in and wants to know who Sam is, and who I am, and when he told him, they fetches me and asks me to make, what did he call it, a formal identification, 'cause I probably knew her better than anyone else.'

'You saw her then?'

Mrs Bywater was about to collapse in tears again, so he poured another brandy and handed it to her. The woman took the glass in her trembling hands but did not drink. It was as if having the drink in her hands was comfort enough.

'I knew the dress straight away. It was her favourite. Quite old it was but she always kept it clean and neat. Then I forced myself to look at her face. It was horrible. So, changed. But I could still tell it were her. And all that lovely brown hair she had, so strong and shiny. Now it had lost its colour and its curls.'

There was silence for a while, then John asked, 'Is she there, still?'

'No. Just after I saw her, they come and took her away. Took her to Shrewsbury, Sam said, so they could do a, what d'you call it, post summat.'

'Post mortem?'

'Ah, that's it.'

There was a pause, then Mrs Bywater stirred and looked about her.

'What am I doing, sitting here, when there's fires to be lit and your breakfast to be made.'

She began to get up but he pressed gently with his hand on her shoulder, telling her to sit down again and tell him more about Miss Owen. She was reluctant at first, but then John settled himself opposite and asked, 'Please. You obviously thought so much of her. Tell me. All that you can.'

TEN

'I'll never forget the day she came to us. 'Bout this time last year, it was. Just a few days afore school started. We'd had the worst summer I ever remember, even worse than this 'un. Harvest was ruined. Mind you, that weren't nothing new. We anna had a decent harvest in years. If it weren't raining fit to bust, it was the gales, pulling the leaves off the trees when they was still green.

'That day were terrible. It had rained from the early hours and it was still raining when she got here. Dark as December by mid-afternoon it was. She was supposed to be here by five thirty, but Jack the carter said her train were an hour late getting in to Shoosbry, then when they got to Longbatch, the valley where Hope Underhill was set, there was this girt tree across the road. Great old ash it were. Took six men to cut through it. When they got to the bottom of the hill, the river had broke its banks, so Jack had to go back up and take the old road down into Hope. Then one of the horses got lame and had to be unhitched, so that slowed 'um down again.

'Luckily, I'd got a good fire going, so when she finally got here, after seven it was, I brought her straight in here to dry. Jack unloaded her luggage, though there weren't much of it. I sat her down in this chair where

I'm sitting now and I thought, well you wunna last long out here, my dear. She looked that young, no more 'n twenty-two or three, and so tired and pale. I could see she was a good-looking lass with her big eyes and all them dark brown curls, but just then she looked as if the wind would blow her over. And I reckoned the children, some of them from off the hill not much better than savages, would break her in a week.

'I couldn't think what the rector was doing bringing her here, especially after the last mistress. Miss Merriweather she were called. Ah, she were merry all right, when she'd had a drop. Kept it in a medicine bottle she did, but I knew what it was. And she sucked these little sweets to try and stop the smell, but it didn't. She'd sit there at the teacher's desk, smilin' and dribblin', quite out of her mind, while the kids played hell about her. School went downhill but the managers kept her on 'cause she was cheap and she never complained about nothing, not even when the offices got flooded and the kids were bringing in you know what on their boots.

'It were difficult to say what age she was, with her face always plastered so thick with powder and rouge but come last July she dropped dead. 'Twas then we found out she were well into her seventies and she weren't a proper teacher at all. Never done no training or nothing. Been a governess to old Lady Bartram over Welshpool way who'd given her a good reference to get rid of her.'

Mrs Bywater paused and looked at John, who had become impatient, but was trying not to show it.

'Just listen to me, rattling on about that silly old Merriweather when you asked me about Miss Owen.' Tears filled her eyes again and she whispered, 'My poor Harriet. How could anyone want to harm her?'

John leaned towards his housekeeper and put his hand over hers for a moment until she was calmed, then asked, 'Where had she come from? Harriet, I mean?'

Mrs Bywater wiped her eyes and continued softly. 'I don't know where exactly. Somewhere up north, I think. Sometimes she said things in a funny way, like *coom* for come and *oop* for up. But when I asked her the name of the place she'd laugh and say, "Oh, Mrs B. — she called me that — you wouldn't like it there at all".'

'So, you didn't think she'd last?'

'Ah, just shows how wrong you can be. That night, I left her sitting in front of the fire, just as she'd been since she come in. She'd hardly spoken at all. I told her she should rest in the morning and I wouldn't disturb her till late. The start of term was still a few days off, so she had time to sort herself out. The last thing I remember of her that night was when she looked up to thank me for my kindness, and it was as if the weight of some awful sadness was weighing her down.'

Mrs Bywater shook her head as she remembered that evening, but then she brightened a little.

'Next day, I kept away till after nine. I remember the church clock chiming just as I were coming out of the house and what a surprise when I come in here. The door was wide open. It was a lovely morning; one of the few good days last September. When I walked in, all her stuff had been unpacked, the furniture had been dusted and polished, even the windows had been cleaned. But Harriet was nowhere to be seen. I called upstairs but there was no answer. Just as I was beginning to wonder what had happened to her, she walked in with an armful of wild flowers. She looked completely different. She had changed her dress; she was wearing a blue one, which showed her fine figure. Her hair was neatly pinned up, but it was so thick and curly you knew it would burst from those pins afore long. Her eyes were sparkling in the sunlight. All the weariness and heaviness of the night before had gone. She was quite small really but standing now with her head thrown back she seemed to have grown a few inches taller. I was quite taken aback by her beauty. Then she saw me looking and frowned.

"Is something wrong?" she asked.

Mrs Bywater smiled at her recollection. "'Not at all," I replied. "I just thought you'd be resting today after your long journey?'

"'On such a lovely morning? Never! There's so much to do. And I like to begin as I mean to go on. You must show me the school room now if you please. I looked for the key but couldn't find it.'"

Mrs Bywater went on. 'I brought the key from its hook in the cupboard under the stairs, where I showed

57

you, Mr Noble, the other day, and opened the door into the school. As I watched her stride before me, I knew two things. One was, she'd have that school under her control within a week and the other, well, I reckoned there'd be a good few men in the village whose hearts would be broken soon enough.' She paused again. 'But I never thought...'

John paused for a moment, then asked, 'If she was as attractive as you say, it's rather surprising that she was unmarried.'

'Yes, I did wonder that myself at first. But she was so determined to run the school well, perhaps she had no time for romance. Anyway, you don't have to take my word for it, I have a photograph. It's in a drawer with a few of her other things. She left in such a hurry that she must have forgotten them. I know 'tis your desk now, sir, but I didn't think you'd mind. I was keeping her bits and pieces just in case.'

Mrs Bywater moved slowly and sadly to the desk and unlocked one of the little drawers inside. John grew impatient to see the picture, although photographs rarely reflected the true beauty of any woman; keeping still for as long as the exposure required usually meant stiffness and a falseness in the expression. At last, Mrs Bywater passed the photograph to him and gazed over his shoulder while he studied it.

There was Miss Owen sitting among a group of her pupils. Several of their faces were blurred because they had been unable to keep still for long enough, but the woman herself sat looking straight at the photographer with remarkable poise. Yes, even in this clumsy, fading, over-exposed image, something of the woman's unselfconscious beauty remained.

'That's strange!' exclaimed Mrs Bywater.

'What is?'

'Well, you see that little locket on the chain around her neck?'

'Yes.'

'She always wore it. Always. But it wasn't round her neck today when I…'

Tears began to rise up again, so John went on quickly, 'Perhaps the doctor or the policemen had removed it.'

'I did ask if there was anything else that might help me to identify her. But they didn't mention the locket, or they chose not to show it to me.'

'Perhaps it was broken when… Perhaps it's still in that field?'

'Yes, that's probably what happened.'

'Would you like me to go and look for it?'

'I don't know. But I do know that it meant a great deal to her, poor woman. She lost it once and got in such a state about it. She was even bad tempered with me, the only time she ever was, and then she thought one of the children might have took it, which was most unlike her. At last, I found it down the side of that chair you'm sitting in now. She was so relieved she give me a kiss and there were tears in her eyes as she went off singing.'

For a moment John thought that Mrs Bywater's own eyes were about to fill with tears again.

'Oh, my goodness, here I am gossiping away and drinking your brandy when you haven't even had your breakfast. Whatever will you think of me.'

John smiled. 'What I think, Mrs B, is that you have been very brave to do what you did this morning, and that you were very fond of Miss Owen and very kind to her. I think that you and I should do our best to find out why her young life was ended so cruelly. Do you agree?'

'Oh, yes sir. For poor Harriet's sake. We must find out what happened.'

ELEVEN

It was mid-afternoon before John could get away from the schoolhouse. In spite of recent events, he would soon be opening the school for the autumn term which involved a great deal of preparation, and he had been interrupted by a visit from Constable Oakes to inform him that he would be required as a witness at the inquest to be held next day in Shrewsbury. Due to the state of the corpse everything was being done as quickly as possible. But, at last, he was able to set off through the village and climb the steep path towards the barley field to search for the locket.

Death was a frequent visitor to Hope Underhill. He usually came with his colleagues, disease and destitution. Mothers, especially in the poorest homes, expected to lose at least one child at birth or during infancy. Sometimes, the mother herself, weakened by hunger and overwork, would lose her life in the difficult process of giving birth, and sometimes the child would be stillborn. And there were regular accidents. In the brief time since his return to Shropshire, John had read in the *Chronicle* of a man crushed by the wheels of his own wagon when his horses took fright at a railway crossing. Even more tragic was the death of a girl, eight years old, left to look after her younger brother and sister while her mother went to work in the fields. She had tried to take down a pan of soup from the hook over the fire when her pinafore caught alight. The flames spread to the rest of her clothing so quickly that by the time her little brother had raised the alarm she was too badly burned to be saved.

The lack of work on the land and the recently increased pay for soldiers had tempted some of the younger men to join the army, and they were sent off to the wars in Zululand or Afghanistan. Some of these men would never return to Hope and lay buried in those far off lands.

But the sudden death of a much liked and admired young woman in such mysterious circumstances was a different matter.

As John walked through the village, past the church, he saw some workmen unloading tools from a cart in preparation for some restoration work. He crossed the old stone bridge and continued along the path beside the outflow from the mill. He had the feeling that the few villagers he saw were trying to avoid him, scurrying indoors or pretending they hadn't seen him, as if he was somehow implicated in Miss Owen's death. This made it even more important for the mystery to be solved as soon as possible.

John was relieved when he left the last cottage behind and the path began to climb steeply towards Long Hill. His path joined the driveway to the manor for a while, but at the once grand, now crumbling, gateway to one of the oldest and largest buildings on this side of the valley, the path forked off and turned into a simple rutted track between the fields. At last, he reached the little field below the wooded slopes, where the squire's gamekeepers raised pheasants and woodcocks for his famous shoots, guarding them vehemently and sometimes violently from trespassers and poachers alike.

The field gate had been left open and as John crossed the stubble, he could see that the reaping machine had been taken away. The last swathe of barley had been left uncut and stood as a memorial to the dead woman. As he approached the place where the young woman had lain, John studied the ground for the locket and chain, but there was no sign of either. When he reached the exact spot where the corpse had been found, he could see the pathway through the barley more clearly than he had the night before, and he began to walk along it. After a few paces, he stumbled on something hidden by the uncut stalks. He bent down and lifted up a smooth round stone that weighed heavy in his hand, and as he turned it over, he noticed a dark stain on one side. John had little doubt that it was dried blood.

He pocketed the stone and continued carefully along the track, pushing the stalks aside and examining the earth below. He followed the line of the trampled path right to the edge of the field. There was nothing else on the ground, but when he reached the fence around the copse, he noticed that the lichen on the top rail had been rubbed off or scratched through in several places, and the grasses below had been trampled. As he peered closely at the marks in the soft green surface, he noticed a tiny piece of blue cloth caught on a bramble trailing the fence. Had the poor girl run through the wood and hurriedly climbed the fence into the field? If so, who or what was she running from? He peered into the copse as if the answer lay somewhere in the blackness between the trees and got the sense that he was being watched.

TWELVE

The coroner's court was held in an ancient building near the town square. Polished oak lined the walls and so little light came in that it was rather like being in a coffin just before the lid was fastened. The coroner, James Howell Esquire, seemed close to death himself, with a skull-like face, a bald head dappled with liver spots, and a few white whiskers lining his cheeks.

Gabriel and the driver could not be released by the farmer as the sun had returned and the harvest work continued apace, so John was the first witness to be called.

'You are?' asked the coroner, loudly, cupping a hand round his left ear, like a trumpet.

'John Noble, sir. Recently appointed master of Hope Underhill National School.'

'Noble?' muttered the coroner. 'Hope Underhill? Would you be related to John Noble, the farmer?'

'His son, sir. My father recently died.'

'Ah!' the coroner exclaimed. 'You were the first person, I believe, to examine the body of the deceased. Would you tell us, in as much detail as possible, what you saw?'

John described what he had seen in the barley field just two afternoons ago. As he described the state of the corpse one or two of the spectators hurriedly left the room. He was followed at the witness stand by Doctor McKenzie, Reverend Whiting and Constable Oakes.

The coroner asked the rector whether the deceased's next of kin had been informed and Whiting explained that none could be found; even the address the deceased had given when appointed as school mistress had proved to be false.

The police surgeon was called next, and John was not surprised to hear that the deceased's skull had been fractured in two places from blows on the back of the head with a heavy object, possibly a large piece of wood or metal, though no fragments of either had been found on the skull. John did not say anything about the stone, because the fractured skull and the heavy blows were enough to inform the coroner of the cause of death and the likelihood of murderous intent. He wanted to continue his own investigations before involving the police.

When all the witnesses had been called and the coroner had briefly retired, John looked around and saw a man sitting at the back of the court he thought he ought to know but could not place. He was tall and broad, about thirty years old perhaps, and handsome in a haughty aristocratic way. He had a florid face and bulging waistline, an indication of too much good living. John wondered who the man was, and what he had to do with the inquest, but his attention was drawn back to the front of the room as the coroner returned.

He cleared his throat and announced in a serious tone, 'Having carefully considered what each witness has said I have decided that the deceased was unlawfully killed by a person or persons unknown.'

There was a slight murmur through the court and a shabby, sickly looking young man with a pencil and notebook in his hand hurried away to get his scoop into the local press.

The coroner glared sourly at the murmurings and movement.

'I believe that to be a suitable verdict and I advise the police to begin serious investigations with the utmost haste.'

Just as everyone was preparing to leave, the police surgeon stood up again and asked the coroner if he might say one more thing. He had forgotten it when he spoke before, or perhaps had not considered it relevant to the case.

'Well, get on with it.'

'I just wanted to add, that when I examined the body, I discovered that the woman was with child. Possibly two months or thereabouts.'

A hubbub arose and the coroner quickly cleared the court.

John left in the company of the doctor and rector, with whom he had travelled to Shrewsbury. He was not travelling back with them, as he wanted to visit some shops and make a brief visit to Aunt Alice. But as they walked together along the High Street, John asked if they had seen the man at the back of the court.

'About my age and height, but much broader and expensively dressed. He disappeared very quickly at the end of the proceedings.'

THIRTEEN

As they walked together across the square Doctor
McKenzie explained that his sight was not what it was
and most things beyond a dozen yards or so were a blur
to him. The rector said that he had been preparing his
sermon during the proceedings and had noticed no one.
He blushed as he spoke and John noticed that he was
trembling again. The thought crossed his mind that the
man might be a secret drinker or perhaps addicted to
laudanum, which would explain the frequent trembling
and the sickly look of his skin, but he had not noticed
any smell of drink or drug on his breath.

They parted and as he walked past the old market
hall John realised how quiet this area of the town had
become since the huge new indoor market hall had been
built a short distance away. He was still thinking about
the stranger in court. There was something vaguely
familiar about him and John couldn't help thinking that
there must be something significant about his
attendance at the inquest.

He started to climb the busy thoroughfare of Pride
Hill. The street was full of shoppers, especially farmers'
wives who had come in to do the weekly shop while
their husbands did business at the livestock market on

the riverside. The main street was crowded at this time of day: pedestrians mingling with carriages and tradesmen's handcarts; a speaker advocating the virtues of the Band of Hope; another announcing the efficacy of Ellerman's Embrocation; a satanic looking individual selling Bibles, and a one-man band entertaining a ragged group of urchins. John called in at the tailor's shop near the top of the hill and was measured for some shirts, then walked down Castle Hill and on to Chester Street where his aunt lived in a smart terraced house with a fine view of the river.

He was pleased to find her well, and now that she had no sick brother to look after she had been able to revive her busy social life. She had read about Miss Owen's murder in the local newspaper and had been shocked that such a thing should happen in Hope Underhill.

'These are bad times, John,' she said. 'Everything is changing for the worse. It is the fault of these Liberals and their interfering reforms.'

After lunch, John walked the short distance to the station to catch the stopping train to Hereford at a quarter past three. When he got off at Churchtown, he would call on Constable Oakes before walking back over Long Hill. Perhaps Oakes would have noticed the man at the back of the court and could tell John who he was.

With a great gasp, the train left Shrewsbury right on time, banging over the iron bridge which crossed the

70

River Severn. Soon, the tracks divided, one set making for the industrial Midlands while the other, carrying his train, headed southwards. They crossed another bridge with a fine view of the ancient, red-stoned Abbey Church. Then the engine began to labour as it climbed up past the village of Meole Brace and the fine escarpment of Lyth Hill. Now the track levelled and their speed increased as they crossed a fertile valley and approached the narrow gorge between the hills where Churchtown was situated.

Leaving the train, John made straight for the constable's office. Oakes was looking very pleased with himself. He waited while John asked about the man he had seen at the inquest and told him that it was Robert Moreton, son of Sir Digby Moreton, the squire of Hope Underhill. While John was digesting this information, Oakes drew himself up to full constabulary dignity.

'I 'appen to have acquired some himportant hinformation,' he said, tapping the side of his nose.

John was still thinking about Robert Moreton and remembering that he had sometimes seen him as a boy when they were both home from school. John wondered if he, himself, had changed that much in the intervening years. His attention was drawn back to the constable by a clearing of the throat before Oakes announced, portentously, 'Gipsies!'

John smiled at himself as he played up the drama of the moment by repeating, 'Gipsies?'

'Ah! Bloody gippos! Camped just the other side of the wood from that there barley field.'

'You think they might have something to do with what happened?' asked John.

'Udden't put it past 'em. Bane of my life is gyppos. If they ain't poachin,' them pinching things off respectable people's washing lines.'

'Yes, but murder? That's a different matter.'

'Well, I ain't saying. But I think we ought to pay 'em a visit, all the same.'

'We?'

'I 'as th'impression you'd like to sort out this nasty business just as much as me. And it wouldn't 'urt for me to take along a witness.'

John thought that this visit to the gipsy encampment would be a waste of time and his thoughts returned to the squire's son.

'I still can't believe that was Robert Moreton. I mean, I only saw him a few times when we were both home from school. And then he was usually galloping past on some expensive looking horse and trampling our hedges down. The last time I saw him he would have been about fifteen or sixteen years old, but he's certainly changed a great deal.'

'The trouble with Robert Moreton,' explained Oakes, 'is he's had too much of his own way. Too much money. Too much time on his hands. If his father popped off, he'd likely buckle down with the estate to see to. But at the present moment, it's gambling, drink and women. And in some respects, he thinks he's above the law. But don't you go thinking he'd 'ave anything to do with poor Miss Owen's murder. He ain't that far gone. And anyways, I don't suppose he even knew her. He's got much fancier fish to fry, like Lady Crumpton's daughter. No, reckon we'd be better off 'aving a word with them gippos.'

'Were you surprised to hear that Miss Owen was with child?'

'That I was. But in some ways, it were to be expected. Fine looking young woman like that. And not married or even engaged to be married so far as I know. Reckon she must have stirred up a good few hearts round 'ere, and stirred up summat else an' all, in some. On the other hand, she seemed so innocent like, and so, how can I put it... in control. I never 'eard she had any special leanings to any man round 'ere. But then I dinna know her that well. Only by sight, like. But she were some sight! Anyways I don't reckon 'er morals had anything to do with her murder.

'No?'

'No! Except I suppose she might have been going to meet someone in some quiet spot when the villain struck. My money's still on them gipsies or some other ragtag and bobtail. Sooner we goes to see 'em the better.'

'Very well. When do you suggest?'

'Tomorrow afternoon?'

73

'It will have to be four o'clock, at the earliest. Miss Owen is being buried at two, and I must speak to the rector after that. The new term begins on Monday and we still have much to sort out.'

'Ah, the Reverend Whiting! Reverend Cold Fish they calls him. Not a popular man by all accounts. They say that all he's interested in is mathematics. Used to teach it up at Oxford apparently. But they wanted to get shot of him, for some reason, so he came to Hope. Losing his congregation fast, I gather, because he wants all that bowing and scraping and incense. Not interested in his parishioners at all, so I've heard.'

'But surely this is just idle gossip?' suggested John, though he was still interested in hearing it. The more he knew about the village where he would soon be teaching, the better.

'Where does idle gossip end and useful information begin?' asked Oakes, with a sly grin, then added, 'Oh, and while we're talking about the reverend, a little bird told me that he were more fond of Miss Owen than perhaps were good for him.'

FOURTEEN

John had so much to ponder on as he crossed Long Hill that he hardly knew how far he had walked, and quite soon he was looking down into the next valley. He took a slight detour to visit his old home and turned south along the track that led to Hillbrow Farm.

The farmhouse itself stood on a terrace overlooking the village about three quarters of a mile below. It was an old house, probably built in Tudor times, out of local stone, with huge chimneys and mullioned windows with leaded panes. The farm buildings and workmen's cottages clustered round it like piglets to a sow and the whole place fitted snugly into the side of the hill behind a windbreak of pines. It had always been a place of warmth and a hive of activity, but as John approached it now, there was no one to be seen; no dogs barked a welcome or a warning; no geese or chickens scattered about the yard. Nothing moved or made a noise except some rooks in the pines.

John rang the bell and knocked on the large, studded door but no one answered. He found one window where the shutters had not been closed and looked inside. When his eyes adjusted to the gloom, he could just make out a small table and low settee.

He had just taken a few steps back to stare at the empty house, when a voice behind him asked, 'Was you looking for someone?'

John turned and saw a man in his fifties standing with a gun under his arm. As soon as the man saw John's face, he lowered the gun and smiled.

'Why, 'tis young Master Noble. I had heard you was back in Hope. It's good to see you and looking so well.'

'You too, George.' He shook the man's hand. 'But what's happened here? Why is there no one about?'

'Place is empty, Master John. Folks as took over when your father left couldn't keep it going. 'Tis a bad time for farming. They did a flit. Now the squire gotta find another tenant.'

'But what about you? Are you still in the cottage?'

'Ah, I'm kept on as a sort of caretaker. Got to keep an eye on the place till a new tenant be found. Marjory and I am grateful for that. At least we got a place to stay and a bit of money coming in. Not like poor old Dick.'

Old Dick, or Richard James as he was properly called, had lived in the other cottage. Richard was his father's favourite workman, and he had been very kind to John as a boy, taking him under his wing, so to speak, and showing him many things his busy father did not have time for, such as how to make and fire a catapult, how to train a dog and ride a pony. Dick always had time for him, even at the end of a long working day.

When John first went to school it was not his parents he missed most, it was Dick James.

John found himself unable to ask, but at last George told him.

'Gone to the work'us, has Dick. In his eighties now. They said he couldn't do for himself no more. Took him away last spring.'

'I see,' John murmured. He said goodbye to George and strode quickly down towards the village, his eyes filling with tears. His aunt was right; everything seemed to be changing for the worse in this part of the world. He began to wonder if it had been wise to return.

FIFTEEN

John spent a restless night, with so many questions turning over in his mind. Why had Harriet Owen written to say she had to leave the village when, in fact, she had not left at all? And if she was still in the district why had no one seen her? What on earth was she doing in the middle of a barley field when she was struck down so cruelly? And if, as Oakes suggested, the squire's son hardly knew her, why had he attended the inquest into her death? Most crucially, who was the father of her baby, and was her pregnancy connected with her murder? Finally, and he felt that this was a vital clue, where was Miss Owen's locket?

Next morning, John went into the schoolroom and looked around, trying to imagine Miss Owen at the teacher's desk, keeping order or marking her pupils' work. There was no sign of a cane, so perhaps she was able to keep order without resorting to physical punishment.

The school had a vaulted ceiling and the windows began above head height. They let in plenty of light, but it would be impossible for most children to see out of them. The whitewashed walls needed a new coat, but generally the place was bright and clean. The school was divided into two rooms, with a glazed partition, now open, in between. The main room was quite large with about thirty double desks. The smaller room was tiered with a long desk and folding seat on each tier so that twenty or so infants could chant the alphabet or multiplication tables under the watchful eye of an assistant or pupil-teacher. It would be one of John's responsibilities to guide a new assistant and help her to pass her examinations so that she could go on to teacher training college. He had not yet met the young girl who would be helping him, as she had gone with her parents to a religious convention at Aberystwyth, and would not be back until Saturday, but he had heard from Mrs Bywater that the girl, aged fifteen, was reliable and competent.

There were the usual pictures on the walls; a map of the world in Mercator's projection, the northern hemisphere seeming so much larger than it actually was, and the British Empire coloured pink. There was also a faded map of the Holy Land. These were standard issues for National Schools. But there were other pictures, much newer and more interesting. One showed a large oak tree with all the creatures who lived on and around it; the other was of a rainbow with its colours identified and an explanation of how this amazing phenomenon was formed. John guessed that these pictures had been ordered by Miss Owen and he felt, as he studied them, that she must have shared his interest in the natural world.

He returned to the teacher's desk and opened the log book, in which the teacher was expected to record significant events and visitors coming to the school. This particular book had obviously been used since the school had opened in 1865 and each incumbent in turn had made entries in their own particular style of handwriting. There had been only four teachers in charge. The first was a Jonathan Wills who wrote in solid copperplate about his achievements in getting pupils into the school and collecting their school pence and administering regular punishments for petty misdemeanours. He lasted almost eight years and was succeeded by another master called William Bamforth who wrote in a huge spidery style so that his shorter stay of three years filled a much larger portion of the book. His entries showed constant dissatisfaction with the school building, the pupils' irregular attendance, their atrocious behaviour and lack of effort. Although not actually stated in the log, John got the impression from the way his entries suddenly broke off, that William's frustrations eventually caused him to leave in high dudgeon or be dismissed.

Next, came the infamous Miss Merriweather, whose handwriting deteriorated considerably during her two years in charge of the school, probably as advancing age and ever more frequent recourse to the "medicine" began to take effect. The only things she bothered to record were visits from important people and the many half holidays they apparently decreed. Also noteworthy during her time were the inspectors' reports, which became increasingly damning, and the consequent drop in payments granted to the school.

Miss Owen had arrived during the terrible weather of September 1878 and that theme monopolised her early entries, written in a neat but informal style.

"Oct 6th: Only seventeen children present today owing to the severity of the weather."

"Oct 27th: A downpour of rain and floods. The outside toilets quite unusable. Sent children home early."

And it was obvious from her entries that a hard winter followed with snow blocking the lanes, keeping the numbers in school low. Illness was another problem, with an influenza epidemic followed by measles. But increasingly Miss Owen's comments were about her pupils; their little successes and general improvement. She recorded a list of the songs they had learned and the difficult arithmetic they had conquered and, in spite of the weather and illness and claims upon them as labourers in the fields, the average attendance, which was entered each week, steadily rose and remained high.

There were some sad entries like the death of a child from pneumonia, and four well-behaved, hard-working children forced to move to another parish when their father was dismissed and evicted for having joined

Joseph Arch's National Agricultural Union. But the overall impression gained from these entries and the reports of the diocesan inspector and Her Majesty's inspectors was of a happy, well run school, where progress was being made in most areas. John was amused by the HMI comments that perhaps the needlework was not of the very highest standard. It was if they were determined to find something negative to comment on. He could not imagine that Miss Owen would have been particularly bothered about that.

As he read through her entries for the past year he began to realise why she had been so much liked and what a tragedy it was that she could not continue as mistress of the school. It would be difficult to follow in her footsteps. He felt himself growing to like Miss Owen, to fall under her spell. But she was dead. Her remains were to be put into the earth that very afternoon.

SIXTEEN

John had agreed that Mrs Bywater should leave a cold lunch for him and then go and prepare herself for the funeral. She had as usual excelled herself with cold meats, home baked bread and her own pickles, but John had no appetite so he wrapped most of the meat in muslin and left it on the cold slab in the pantry for later.

The bell began to toll as John made final adjustment to his dress. Then he crossed the school yard, passed through the lych gate and walked up the path. He glanced at the fading flowers on his parents' graves and realised that he had neglected them in recent days. Miss Owen's grave waited, open, just a few yards to the left, its newly lifted soil glinting in the watery sunlight. Beyond her grave stood a row of juniper bushes and John noticed several small figures hiding behind their dark fronds, but he had no time to investigate because the bell had stopped tolling and he must hurry along.

The sunlight outside barely penetrated the narrow, stained-glass windows of the church, and when John entered, he felt the chill of cold stone. He slid into a pew at the back and studied the congregation. There were few mourners. It had proved impossible to contact any of Miss Owen's family or anyone at all who knew her before she came to the village. The rector had, at first, refused to give Miss Owen a Christian funeral, but an anonymous donor had provided enough money to cover the cost, along with a handsome gift to the church, on the understanding that she be placed in a decent coffin and buried with proper ceremony. The unborn child was removed and placed in unconsecrated ground just beyond the churchyard, among the graves of children who had not lived long enough to be received into the church.

At the front, near the coffin, stood a couple of well-dressed, middle-aged gentlemen, probably school managers, John thought. He had not been introduced to them, but he recognised them as important men of the village. Just behind them stood Mrs Bywater, weeping into a large handkerchief. As John looked at her tear-stained face he remembered their painful conversation earlier that morning.

'I don't believe it. I simply don't believe. Harriet would never have…'

'But it is a fact, Mrs B. A horrid but irrefutable fact,' said John.

'How dare they open her up like that! It's not natural!'

'Did you never suspect she had a lover?'

'I know she didn't. I never saw her show any more than her usual friendliness with any man. I knew that girl better than I know my own daughter.'

'Look, I know this is painful, Mrs Bywater. But if we are ever to discover who killed her we must look at all the facts, even the most surprising and uncomfortable facts.'

'I suppose so,' Mrs Bywater conceded.

'Think back to last summer,' said John. 'Did Miss Owen change her behaviour in any way?'

'Well, when summer come, it seemed to lift her spirits. Mind you, she were generally a cheerful soul. But I remember her saying how much she had come to love the valley. She began to go for long walks in the evening. She would take a notebook with her and jot down things about the countryside and press flowers in her book and bring back birds' feathers and such like so that she could identify them later. Sometimes when she come home, she looked so happy and healthy. Her face really glowed. Sometimes it were quite dark when she got back and I wasn't happy about that. Told her, I did, it weren't right for a young woman to be on her own in the fields and woods when it got dark. If only I'd known what was going to 'appen I'd 've *made* her come home earlier.'

'But she was a grown woman, Mrs B. You couldn't have told her what to do.'

'Well, I'd 've bloody well tried.'

Mrs Bywater was probably the only person in church who was close to Harriet Owen. Spread around the nave were several pale, shabby, elderly women who generally attended funerals just to pass the time and come to grips with the inevitable. Most of the villagers could not afford to take time off work or leave their young families even for the funeral of a well-respected school mistress. Then, as John looked around, he saw Robert Moreton sitting quietly at the back of the church.

The rector began the ceremony. John could see at once why he was not liked as a preacher. He hardly glanced up from his prayer book as he delivered the words of the service in an affected, unfeeling monotone. Actually, the man looked ill. His face was thin and grey and his eyes sunken, making him look much older than his fifty or so years. His eulogy was brief, entirely factual and delivered to a spot somewhere near his feet.

Soon enough the service ended and the coffin was lifted with very little effort by the undertaker's men and carried outside to the grave. John followed the small party of mourners and looked for Robert Moreton, but he had disappeared. In just a few minutes, the burial was complete and the mourners began to drift away. John walked around the churchyard. He would give the rector a few minutes to disrobe before meeting him in the vestry as arranged.

He had reached the lych gate when he glanced back and saw a dozen children, boys and girls, aged from about four years old to twelve, march out in single file from behind the junipers towards the open grave. Each one threw in a small posy of wild flowers, then they stood in a circle round the grave while the oldest girl said a short prayer. All the children joined in *amen*, before leaving the way they had come.

FOURTEEN

When John returned to the church, Sam Bywater, the sexton, was already busy filling his spade from the heap of soil alongside the grave and clattering it onto the coffin. John remembered how some of the African tribes would carry their dead out into the jungle where jackals and other scavengers would clean away the flesh in hours. He thought, in many respects, it was a superior way of dealing with death, but here, there was no jungle and no jackals. Nevertheless, it seemed strange to encase bodies in expensive wood and bury them deep in the earth, when the outcome was the same. *Earth to earth, ashes to ashes, dust to dust.* The body would decompose and eventually even the bones would crumble away. It was the natural end for all unless the body was cremated. John no longer believed in any sort of resurrection. The only way a person would live on would be in the memories of others, like those children remembering their beloved teacher. And how long would they go on remembering her?

The church door was half open so John slipped inside and stood looking at the altar. He thought of all the time he had spent in places like this, the Sunday visits to this church as a child, the daily hour in chapel when he was away at school, the services at Cambridge, and all sorts of places during his training as a missionary. He was ordained in a grand cathedral and was sent out to pray the same prayers and sing the same hymns in a wooden hut in the middle of Africa, with just a handful of native people in the congregation.

Standing in the silence, John became aware of a low wailing and sobbing coming from the vestry. It stopped when he knocked on the door. There was a pause and a strange shuffling before the rector asked him to come in. Whiting was sitting in a heavy chair at the vestry table, still wearing his vestments, with a Bible open in front of him, which appeared to be upside down. The rector closed the holy book, quickly turned it round the right way and asked John to sit down.

'Look,' began John. 'If you would prefer another time…'

There was a pause while the rector regained his composure.

'The truth is that Miss Owen's death has affected me a great deal.'

'That's not surprising. After all, it was you who recommended her for the post and you probably saw a good deal of her, as correspondent for the managers and a frequent visitor to the school.'

'Yes, but…' The rector paused again.

He was a broken man. His thin greying hair hung lank about his sunken cheeks. His eyes were red and swollen. There was a look of despair in them.

'I never had much time for women, except my mother of course. I saw them as silly creatures who would get in the way of my career. I never met a woman who showed the least interest in mathematics and I wanted so much to achieve something significant in that field. The last thing I needed was a wife who would demand my attention and distract me with petty concerns. And then there might be children… oh no. But I was a man… I had my… needs. I used to visit a woman in Oxford. She began to see me as a good catch. Marriage to a clergyman and professor would establish her respectability. When I broke off the relationship, she went to the head of my college and told him everything. He didn't make much fuss. He found this living for me and told me to leave as soon as possible. So, I came here and hated it from the beginning.

'I had been here for three years. The worst years of my life. I saw no way out. I even considered ending it, except that would have been a sin. Then she came.'

'You mean Miss Owen?'

'Yes, Harriet. From the first time I saw her I fell foolishly in love. It was ridiculous. An old man like me utterly captivated by a pretty young woman. But each time I saw her I became more infatuated.

'Before long, I knew that I had to ask her to marry me. Of course, she was not of my social class. My mother would have been horrified, God rest her soul. And I knew that Harriet had no romantic feelings for me. Why would she? An old man like me. But I could have given her a better life, a grander home. I would have been a generous, attentive husband. She would have grown to love me. After all, she was alone and unmarried. She did not seem to have any special admirers or suitors, not even a close friend. Of course, we know differently now. There was someone, someone with whom she did unspeakable things.'

The rector shivered as he said this and held his breath as if resisting the urge to vomit.

'And who planted his seed in her without God's blessing and gave her that unborn bastard...'

Whiting paused, trying to control his feelings.

'If only I had spoken earlier, I might have saved her from sin. It wasn't until Whitsun that I finally plucked up the courage to propose and do you know what happened? She thanked me for my kind offer, told me that my proposal was very flattering, said that she liked me a little, but that she could never marry me and she asked me never to mention it again.

'I felt as if my life had ended. I didn't try to see or speak to her again. Then she disappeared! The next time I saw her she was dead in that barley field.'

Suddenly, he straightened up and looked at John in horror.

'I don't know why I am telling you all this. After all, I hardly know you.'

'I think you had to tell someone. And I would never betray your confidence.'

'Yes, perhaps you are right. Thank you.'

'Now it is my turn to make a confession,' began John. 'I know that the death of this young woman is not really my concern. But perhaps because I have taken her position, or because I was one of the first to see her corpse…'

The rector covered his face with his hands and moaned.

'Or simply because her young life was ended in such a horrible way…'

Another cry came from behind the rector's hands.

'Whatever the reason, I am determined to find out what happened. I know the police are carrying out their own investigations but I have little faith in them. I want to find out what happened myself. So, will you tell me anything that might help?'

'Of course, but I don't see how…'

'Well, for instance, you say that everyone liked her. Can you think of anyone, anyone at all, that she might have upset?'

'No, no one. Except…'

'Except?'

'Well, there was one parent. A local farmer. Man called Hughes. A belligerent man at the best of times; he has been rude to me on several occasions. Miss Owen wanted his son to stay on at school; she believed that the boy was very bright. But the farmer was adamant his son must leave the school as he was needed on the farm. The discussion became quite heated, I believe.'

'What happened to the boy?'

'Well, of course, he left the school at the end of term. He was old enough and had achieved the required standard, so he could not be compelled to remain.'

'Miss Owen left it at that?'

'Unfortunately not. She continued to pester Hughes. Visited his farm. I am told that he threatened her.'

'Hmm! I must speak to him. But I hardly think it would have been cause enough for him to murder her. Anyone else?'

'There's the squire's son, Robert.'

'Robert Moreton? What about him?'

'It was just after Easter. He appeared at a managers' meeting and told them that they must get rid of Miss Owen at once. He said he had learned things about her that made her unsuitable for the post. But when pressed, he refused to give any details. Then he suddenly changed his mind. Went off in a bluster, saying we could keep the damn woman. He never came to us again. It was most peculiar.'

'Perhaps that has something to do with his attendance at the inquest, and her funeral.'

'I didn't notice him myself. But perhaps you're right.'

'I must speak to Robert Moreton as soon as possible.'

'Well do take care. He's a powerful man. His father is the most important landowner in the valley so you don't want him to take against you. He is a benefactor to the village and to the church. He has made a large donation to the cost of the restoration work you may have noticed going on. And he has considerable influence with the managers. It was largely his money that built the school.'

There had to be a link between Robert Moreton and Miss Owen. If John could discover what it was, he might be able to solve the mystery.

Suddenly, John remembered his appointment with Oakes. He drew out his watch and realised that Oakes would be arriving at the schoolhouse in a few minutes.

'I must leave you now, Reverend. I'm sorry we haven't got far with school affairs, but perhaps we can meet tomorrow, if you can spare the time.'

'We must find the time. Your pupils will be arriving the day after tomorrow. We must not get so distracted by this other business that we are not ready to receive them. I will come to the schoolhouse at ten o'clock tomorrow.'

'Of course. But about this other matter. Can I make one further request? Could I see the letter Miss Owen wrote to the managers explaining her sudden departure?'

'I believe that the letter is still in the minute book. I will bring it with me tomorrow. And thank you for hearing me out. I feel much relieved to have been able to tell someone about my feelings. You are sure my confidences will go no further?'

John gave him a firm assurance on that score. They left the vestry together. As John crossed to the south door he glanced back and saw the Reverend Whiting on his knees in front of the altar: a man who desperately needed his God.

FIFTEEN

John followed Oakes up the side of the hill, trying to match the young constable's stride, but soon falling several paces behind. At least Oakes was in no mood to talk so John had time to consider the information the rector had given him. He had been astonished by the Reverend Whiting's revelation of his infatuation with the young teacher. He found it hard to believe that such an old man — he did seem quite old to John who had just reached his thirtieth year — could have had such passionate feelings. But the admission of those feelings to a comparative stranger seemed to exonerate him. The young woman had rejected his proposal of marriage, but not unkindly, and they seemed to have parted amicably, so it was unlikely that the rector had been the one to deal the fatal blow.

It was far more possible that the murderer might be Robert Moreton. How strange was that visit to the managers' meeting. What on Earth could he have found out about Miss Owen to make him describe her as unsuitable for the post, especially when everyone else had such a good opinion of her capabilities? And why fail to support his assertion with any details? But that had all happened several months ago and could hardly be connected with the recent tragedy. There was some mystery about their relationship, John was sure of that, and he felt that he should be interviewing Robert Moreton, rather than following Oakes on this futile visit to the gipsy encampment.

It was the second week of September and the evenings were closing in, so by the time the men had turned off the road and begun to cross the fields towards the copse, the sun was slipping behind Devil's Peak and the hedges and trees were casting long, cool shadows. Soon, the sun disappeared completely and dusk began to thicken. When they reached the trees, they did not enter the copse but followed it around on the eastern side where the heather covered moorland of Long Hill began. It wasn't long before they saw the encampment, five caravans in a semicircle around a fire, above which a large iron pot hung from a tripod of sturdy hazel sticks.

Even in the fading light the caravans looked splendid, with their carved wood and brightly painted panels. A group of horses stood nearby feeding from a pile of hay. Beside the fire sat a group of children, dipping hunks of bread into some sort of broth. A tall, thin woman with dark skin and black hair tended the fire while an older woman sat on a step between the lowered shafts of her caravan, smoking a long clay pipe. Framed in the doorway of another van was a third woman, not much more than a girl, but already tall and stately. She half closed the curtains across the entrance as John and Oakes drew close. There were no men to be seen. They were probably somewhere deep in the copse, finding the next day's meat.

Oakes drew himself up to his full height in front of the oldest woman. 'Good evening, Hepzibah.'

The woman removed the long pipe from her mouth, spat some phlegm accurately into the fire, then stared straight at the young policeman.

'Well, if it ain't young Constable Oakes, come to see us again.'

During this exchange one of the children, a boy of eight or nine, slipped quietly away from the fire and made for the trees.

The old woman began to refill her pipe as she spoke. 'And who's this pretty gentleman you'm brought with you? 'e looks a might too smart to be a gamekeeper and a bit too young to be a magistrate. But now I gets a proper look I reckon I do know him.'

'My name is Noble. John Noble. You used to camp on my father's land when I was a boy.'

'Ah, that's it. Got a strong look of your father, you 'ave. We was all sorry when he give up the farming. Good man he were. Never minded us stopping fer a while. Understood our ways. I did hear that the poor man had passed away. Is that so?'

John confirmed this while Oakes cleared his throat impatiently.

'Mr Noble is the new master of the school in Hope. Since Miss Owen met her untimely death.'

The old woman was so shocked at these words that the pipe dropped from her lips. A little girl quickly retrieved it, then sat on the shaft beside Hepzibah.

'Dead! You say she's dead?'

A man emerged from the dark trees, followed by another and another, then came the boy who had gone to fetch them. The first man carried a heavy looking staff which he lifted in a threatening manner. But the old woman spoke softly.

'No need of that, Sean. The man brings terrible news.'

By now the whole party had gathered round, their faces flashing in the firelight as the darkness deepened.

Oakes told them all what had happened. There were murmurs from the men and keening among the women. One of the men, probably the one called Sean, spoke.

'You say this dreadful thing were done in that barley field, t'other side of this wood. When did this 'appen?'

'We cannot be exactly sure,' John explained. 'The body was found three days ago. But it might have been lying there for several days before that.'

The murmurs grew louder and there were soft cries from the women. Oakes stood tall and crossed his thick arms over his chest.

'So, you see what we'm looking for is a murderer. A man, or a woman I suppose, if she were strong made, who felled that poor young woman and left her for dead.' He looked round at them all, then asked, 'You were camped here at that time?'

Hepzibah replied, 'Aye, we canna deny it. Been 'ere three weeks or more. But we didn't have no dealings with that harvest field. Our 'elp ain't needed these days.'

Another woman spoke. 'There was one man who wangled his way into the harvest field. Not really one of us. He only stayed a few days. On his way south he said.'

'Oh, ah,' interrupted Sean. 'A strange one he was. Big strong fella. Turned up late one evening and asked to stay a couple of days. Paid his way he did. Not short of money. Made himself friendly with the ladies, I believe.'

As he spoke Sean looked across at the younger woman who had come to sit at the front of her van. She got up quickly and went inside.

Hepzibah continued the tale. 'Good looking chap. No doubt about it. Spoke a bit foreign, I thought. Could sing too. Gave us a few tunes most evenings. Stayed with us a while. Slept under one of the vans. Then one morning he was gone.'

Oakes grew agitated, perhaps thinking that he'd found his man and lost him again all in one moment.

'This passing stranger, did he have a name?'

A girl's voice came from inside the caravan. 'Antonio. But he liked to be called Tony.'

'And when did he leave?' asked Oakes.

There was silence for a moment. These people did not bother much with counting the days. But again, the voice came from the caravan. 'Six nights ago.'

Several of the group had sat down by now; the men with pipes lighting them with faggots from the fire, the women drawing shawls about their shoulders as the night grew chill.

Oakes was preparing to leave when Hepzibah spoke loudly. 'About a week ago you say. Was the moon full then, Violet?'

The girl came out again from the caravan; her face pale in the glow of a rising quarter moon.

'Aye, Grandmother, it were.'

'Then that were the night I saw Black Powell's chariot on the lost road.'

Oakes stirred impatiently. He had no time for fairy tales.

'Well, I must be off back to the office and get a message to Shrewsbury. This man must be caught, wherever he might be.' He turned to the slender woman by the fire. 'Going south you said? Six days? That means he could be past Gloucester by now. Are you coming, John?'

'You let him stay awhile. I likes the look of him,' said Hepzibah.

John hesitated. It was late, and he had much to do. But he was fascinated by the old woman's talk of Black Powell's chariot.

'You go on, Constable. But let me know if or when you catch up with that man.'

'Right. I'll bid you all good night. For once we part as friends. But if I catch...' Then he saw Sean's staff and went on his way.

When Oakes was out of sight, Hepzibah shouted orders to the men to light the lanterns on the vans and to the women to fetch eating bowls. One of the children brought a box for John to sit on. Then he was served with broth from the pot over the fire and a jug of cider. There was something of rabbit in the broth along with potatoes and herbs and it tasted good.

'You were telling us about Black Powell's chariot,' John reminded her. 'Who was he and why was he called Black Powell?'

The old woman paused, sucking her pipe into a fierce glow. The others gathered close.

Hepzibah sucked on her pipe again, then explained. 'Because he was always diggin' under the ground, him and all his tribe. They dug up gold and silver and copper and lead. Out of the mountain sides. And they spent so long down there in the dirt that it got into their skin and turned them black.'

Another pause while her audience settled themselves.

''Tis a tale I learned off my mother when I was a girl and she had learned it off her mother years 'afore that. You see there's an old road comes across the hills just north of Hope, then climbs up near where the squire lives now, went right through this 'ere wood and on across the hill. That road were made long before there were squires and rectors and villages like Hope. Even before them Romans came and made their long straight streets. You can hardly trace that old road now. But I know where it comes from and where it goes. It was made by the people who lived beyond the Devil's Peak, in the high mountains over that way. They used it when they came to trade or make war with the tribes who lived further east.

'Black Powell was one of their most powerful chiefs. But he had a weakness for women. Whenever he discovered a beautiful young woman, he had to have her. What he could not get by the attraction of his title or the splendour of his court he would take by force.'

She broke off for a moment, as all good storytellers do, and offered John more cider which he accepted and quickly drank down, waiting for the old woman to continue with her tale. But first, she beckoned to the women to take the smallest children, one of whom was already sleeping, off to bed.

There was a tremendous stillness now the little ones were gone. The moon had also disappeared behind a mist that was rising from valley below, as it often did at this time of the year. The fire was stirred to a new brightness which made the darkness beyond appear impenetrable. It became easy to imagine those distant times when wolves, and worse, still prowled these hills.

'Black Powell's problems began when he fell in love. He had discovered the most beautiful maiden, the daughter of another chieftain living to the north of his domain. She was sixteen, willow slim, with hair the colour of ripe corn. But it was her eyes that drew men to her. Deep blue-green like the lakes among the mountains that surrounded her home, so that when you looked into them you felt you were falling in and would gladly drown.'

John looked at the old woman's face, thin and deeply lined, but the high bones of her cheeks and the strength of her brow were remnants of the beauty she must once have been. She stretched out her thin wrists, heavy with bangles, sighed and went on with her story.

'Black Powell asked for the girl's hand in marriage, but she was already betrothed to another chieftain's son, who was only a little older than herself, handsome and brave. She would have none of Black Powell and her father supported her refusal, even though the link with Powell's tribe would have given him a powerful ally.

'Now, Black Powell was not a man to be refused anything. He attacked the other tribe and slaughtered them all, man woman and child, burning their township to the ground. But the girl had escaped on the back of her betrothed's best horse.'

The old gipsy stopped for a moment to scratch at something in her hair. There were things flying about in the night air, drawn to the firelight.

'Black Powell discovered which way the young couple had gone. They were making for the flatter lands to the east where long settled tribes led more civilised lives. But when they got to the plain, they discovered that the great rivers there were in flood so they had to come south to cross these hills.

'At last, they reached the Devil's Peak and the young couple thought they were far enough ahead to rest. They made a bodily thing of their love, slept among the tumbled stones and in the first light they saw the road ahead, crossing the hills to the east. Unfortunately, the horse that had carried them both so far yesterday had stumbled in the dusk and was too lame to go on. They must continue their journey eastward on foot.'

Hepzibah paused again and sniffed the air as if she anticipated a change in the weather, then went on.

'A thickening sky, lurid with the rising sun, showed a gathering storm. We all know that rain in these parts comes from the west, but the worst winter storms are always blown from the east. Then they heard a horn sound behind them and saw Black Powell's chariot, pulled by two black stallions, just a few miles away.

'The sky was lowering minute by minute and by the time they reached the bottom of the valley where Hope Underhill now stands the snow had begun to fall and the river had flooded, freezing their legs as they stumbled through the sticky mire. At mid-morning, it was almost as dark as night. By the time they reached the top of the hill, near where we are now, the wind was blowing the snow straight into their faces but luckily the wind would not let the snow settle and instead whirled it into deep drifts against any obstruction or filled any hollows, so they were still just able to see where the road ahead went.'

Hepzibah began to rock gently backwards and forwards in rhythm with her words. John felt himself falling asleep but wanted to hear the rest of the tale.

'When Black Powell reached the top of Devil's Peak he found their horse and smelled their lovemaking. This increased his rage and he drove his chariot too fast downhill, getting the wheels stuck in the marsh. The horses were thrashed fiercely, to draw the chariot out again, but the lovers were safely over the top of Long Hill by the time Black Powell reached it.'

Again, she sniffed the air as if to foretell the weather.

'By now, the wind had dropped, the snow had settled knee deep, and the road had disappeared. The huge flakes ambling thickly down made it impossible to see ahead more than a few paces.

'Black Powell became deranged. He thought he saw a light ahead. He pointed into the curtain of snow, saying that he could see the girl's hair shining in a beam of sunlight. He whipped on the horses and sent them flying across the snow-covered hilltop. But he had left the road and suddenly the ground dropped away, cliff-like, into a deep valley. Black Powell and his chariot were smashed on the rocks below.'

The old woman stopped and smiled broadly at the satisfying justice of the ending, but then added an intriguing coda.

'The strange thing is, that in the next valley there was no snow and the sun was shining, but this light had led Black Powell to his doom. And it is said that sometimes at a full moon, when the place is bathed in moonlight, his chariot can be seen hurrying across the top of the hill.'

It had been a long day and the cider was wickedly strong. John did not fight the sleep that overcame him as he slipped from his seat and lay beside the fire. He knew nothing of the strong arms that lifted him gently into the old woman's van. He was racing across the mountain in a gig with a young woman beside him. But she was not a corn haired beauty from some ancient legend; she was a mouldering corpse in a pale blue dress.

SIXTEEN

Mrs Bywater was horrified when John stumbled in, very pale, holding his head in his hands, just before nine.

'Oh, my Lord, you looks a sorry sight, Mr Noble. Where 'as you been?'

'Don't fuss, Mrs B. Just make me some strong tea. Oakes and I were out late last night, following up a lead. I spent the night at his office, in the cell, on a very hard bed.'

John was astonished how readily the lies came to him, but they were not really lies, just slight distortions of the facts.

'I'll just wash and change while the tea's brewing. The rector will be here at ten. It's our last chance to discuss the school before it opens on Monday.'

John tried to rush away so that he could splash some water on his face and lie down for a while, but Mrs Bywater was intrigued.

'And did you find any answers? You must tell me. You did say we were in this together.'

'Well, it seems there was a stranger around at the time. Staying with the gipsies near the field. Now he's disappeared. Oakes has begun the hunt for him.'

'That's not surprising. Lots of things disappear when there's gippos about.'

'Now, Mrs B., that's just unreasonable prejudice.'

'How long were you with these gipsies, Mr Noble? If you don't mind my asking?'

'Just long enough to ask a few questions. Oh, and to hear an old story about some lost road.'

'Were you offered anything to eat or drink?'

'Just a little stew and a cup of cider.'

'Ah, that explains it. They puts mushrooms in that stew. Special sort of mushrooms, that only they knows where to find.'

'I see,' said John, remembering the many strange potions he had been offered in Africa and the weird effects these sometimes had.

When John removed his clothes, he found that some loose change was missing from his pocket and in its place was a small bag of lavender. As he sniffed the purple flowers, he decided that it was trade, rather than theft, and nobody's business but his own.

He had recovered a little by ten o'clock when the rector arrived. Reverend Whiting looked as if he had not slept for a week nor bothered to change his clothes.

'My housekeeper has deserted me,' explained the rector. 'She asked for a better wage and I refused, of course. She called me a hypocrite! Told me I needed God more than any of my parishioners. I have advertised for a replacement, but in the meantime…'

'Perhaps we should postpone our discussion.'

'No. It's our last chance. I shall be busy with services all day tomorrow. It would not be fair to let your pupils arrive without warning you.'

'Warning me?'

'Discipline! Many of these children come to school unwillingly and only want to learn enough to reach the required standard so that they can leave school at the earliest opportunity. They must be kept in control at all times. Spare the rod, spoil—'

'There doesn't seem to be a rod…'

'Ah, I see. Well, that was Harriet's… Miss Owen's way. She would not use physical punishment. Kept on about some damned Swiss fellow whose ideas on education she followed. He had a strange foreign name, Pesta something, I think it was. She had the cane locked away. But I have the key.'

'Could she really manage to keep order without threatening the cane?'

'Apparently. I warned her about it again and again. I reminded her that these youngsters were full of original sin. It must not be allowed to flourish. God had ordained their place and they must be taught to keep it. But she would not listen. "Let me do it my way," she would say.'

The rector paused, his mouth twitching and his body trembling with some barely controlled feeling. Then he abruptly changed the subject.

'Attendance! The parents will find any excuse to keep their children at home. Bad weather! Illness in the family! Needed in the fields! No boots to wear! No boots indeed! They could all have new boots if the fathers didn't spend their wages on drink.'

The rector's anger at least brought some colour back to his grey cheeks.

'You must insist on good attendance, John. If they do not attend, they cannot learn. And we must impress the inspectors, or the grant will be reduced. Results are everything. And we cannot improve the results if the pupils fail to attend. Note the malingerers, John. Write to the parents. Visit them if you can. Insist on absence notes. Keep at them.'

'The log book shows that attendance has improved.'

'Exactly! And the managers will want to see that improvement continued. They will be watching you very carefully, and they will be watching me too. I took the responsibility of appointing you and if things go wrong, I will be blamed. They would never have found a replacement in time had it been left to them, but they will still blame me, just as they blame me for Miss Owen's sudden disappearance. They will be watching you very carefully indeed.'

'But how can they blame you for Miss Owen's disappearance? Oh, by the way, you promised to let me see her letter.'

'I have it here. Please keep it safe.' He handed John the folded sheet, which he pocketed.

'Mrs Bywater tells me that you appointed Miss Owen in similar circumstances.'

'Yes, I was under pressure to find someone in a hurry. Has Mrs Bywater mentioned Merriweather?'

John nodded.

'The silly woman dropped dead just a fortnight before the school was due to reopen. I saw to it that an advertisement was placed in the press, but there were no suitable applicants. Then I remembered that a friend of mine from Oxford days was now the principal of a new teacher training college near Manchester and he might just know of an ex-student who was not yet placed. He wrote back immediately to tell me about this young woman, who had been very successful in her first school, but had been forced to leave, by illness in her family, I think it was. She had recently written to him to say that she was now able to teach again but had been unable to find a suitable post in the area where she now lived. He said he would contact her and he would send me a testimonial which he was sure I would find encouraging and he would ask her previous school to send on a reference. So, it all happened very quickly. I recommended Miss Owen to the managers. A week later she arrived. Strangely that other reference never came, but by the time I had got round to worrying about that, the new term had begun and the managers were already impressed with the new mistress.

'I see,' John muttered, thinking that everything about his predecessor seemed slightly mysterious.

'Now, let us think about the new term. Firstly, the pupil-teacher, Agnes Beale has returned from Aberystwyth, with her family, and will be attending the morning service, so I will introduce you to her afterwards. She is very competent, I can assure you. You will need to arrange for her own lessons, so that she can take her examinations at the end of the year. I shall be coming into the school once a week to give the pupils their religious instruction. I would prefer to continue my practice of coming on Friday morning. The rest of the details, such as the register and lighting the stoves and the payment of your salary we will leave for a later meeting.'

Suddenly, he stood up.

'Now, I must leave you. I have another appointment. I wish you well, for your sake and mine. God be with you.'

The recent animation left his face. He looked at John with haunted eyes and hurried away.

SEVENTEEN

There was just one more thing John wanted to do before the new term began, so after lunch he set off in the drizzle to walk up Hunger Hill towards the workhouse. This was by far the newest and ugliest building in the valley and in the gloomy afternoon, its starkness, standing alone on a grassy slope about a mile from the village, seemed particularly forbidding. The Longbatch Union served a wide area and in normal times such a huge building would not have been justified for a scattering of tiny hamlets, isolated farms and cottages. But at present, due to the depressed state of agriculture, the place was full.

As John approached the tall, square block of blue brick and grey slate he shuddered, not just in the chill, late September air, but with sympathy for anyone who might have the misfortune to be incarcerated in such a place.

He had learned from the newspapers that after the scandal at the Andover Workhouse, where the paupers had been reduced by hunger to gnawing the rotting bones they had been set to pound, a more humane regime had been advocated by the commissioners, but, as usual, such new ideas took longer to reach outlying districts such as the Welsh Marches.

John entered the workhouse and asked to speak to the guardian, but he was told he was very busy at present, so John must wait in the passage outside his quarters. After about half an hour John decided to wait no longer. He knocked loudly on the heavy oak door and walked in. A portly middle-aged man sat at a large table eating an enormous meal. His face reddened at the interruption, but as soon as he noted that his visitor was well-dressed and well-spoken, he manoeuvred his bulk out from his chair and stood.

'My dear sir, I am so sorry to have kept you waiting. I thought you were another applicant. We have so many these days.'

He wiped his greasy hands on his coat tails and came forward with his hand outstretched, but John kept his at his side.

'My name is Noble, John Noble. My father was the tenant of Hillbrow Farm until he retired. You have one of his workers in your care, I believe. Mr Richard James.'

'Ah, James. Yes. One of our more amenable paupers.'

'A good worker and a good man.'

'Of course,' said the guardian, with a flicker of a smile.

'I trust I shall find him in good health and spirits. I have brought him a gift.' John presented the basket

115

containing one of Mrs Bywater's delicious pies and a bottle of ale.'

'Very good. If you leave that with me, I shall make sure he receives it.'

'That will not be necessary. If you tell me where Mr James can be found I will deliver it personally.'

The guardian's face reddened again. 'Oh, I'm afraid we don't allow...' but when he saw the look on John's face, he changed his mind. 'Well, generally we don't, but in the circumstances. You will find J... Mr James in room seven.'

He turned to pick up a large bell from the table, saying, 'I will ask one of our more capable paupers to show you the way.' But John had already left.

The corridors seemed endless, but at last he found the place; a large high-ceilinged room with beds crammed in along the walls, with no sign of any tables, drawers or lockers where the paupers might keep any personal belongings. Some very elderly or infirm inmates lay in their beds, others sat on the bed ends, with their heads bowed, not even bothering to look up as John passed by. The room was thick with the odours of sweat, intestinal gases and carbolic. Another group of men leaned against the wall near the door, all dressed in the same ill-fitting clothes, all unshaven.

John approached them and asked, 'Can you tell me where I can find Mr James? Dick James?'

When John spoke, one of the men jumped, as if he expected words to be followed by blows. Another, seeming to take an age to realise that John had spoken, to understand the words, and to form an answer, at last, pointed through the door.

John thanked the man and went outside into a small yard, where an old man sat alone on a bench, partly sheltered from the drizzle by the small overhang of an upper storey. He was dressed in the same institutional uniform and his face had the same unshaven look as the men inside, but his posture remained erect and there was a glint in his eyes.

'Why, 'tis Master John,' he said, struggling to his feet and smiling briefly. ''Ave you come to take me home?'

John took the old man's hands in his; they were cold and rigid as stone.

'I'm afraid I can't do that, Dick. But now I know where you are, I shall visit often.'

'Of course, I remember now. I don't have a home no more. Not since your father gave up the farm and them as came after him cleared off.'

'But, Dick, weren't you supposed to move into one of the alms houses by the church?'

'Ah, that's what the old rector had arranged, but it seems he dain't put nothing in writing, and the new fella, what's his name?'

'Whiting.'

'That's right. When I went to claim the key from him, he said he'd given the house to someone in greater

117

need. He was in a bad temper, he weren't happy at all that I'd interrupted.'

'Interrupted what, Dick?'

'I'm not sure, but he were in the vestry with the new schoolmistress. His face was purple, and the young woman seemed glad to get away.'

'Did you know that she was dead?'

'I 'eard summat about that. And I'm right sorry.'

John felt the warmth gradually creeping back into the old man's hands. 'Why do you stay out here in the cold and drizzle, Dick?'

The old man lowered himself slowly back onto the bench, saying, ''Cause I've been outside all my life. I canna bear to be in there. All crowded in.' He drew in a deep breath. 'At least they canna stop me breathin' But tell me, Master John, what brings you back to Hope?'

'I came for my father's funeral. Did you know he had died, Dick?'

'Ah, I did 'ear. I wanted to go to the funeral, but I can't walk that far no more.'

'Why didn't you ask the guardian to arrange transport for you?'

'I wouldn't ask that man to lift me if I were lying in the midden.'

John smiled. He was pleased that not all of Dick's spirit had faded.

'Are you well looked after here, Dick?'

'I looked after the animals better when I was able. I'm just glad my Annie went afore I had to come in 'ere.

It would have broke her heart. I remember the words at our wedding, *those as God 'as joined together, let no man put asunder,* but in 'ere they does just that. Men in one place; women in another. But 'tis the only place for me now, Master John. I can't work no more. My bit of savings is long gone. But I'm eighty-four this year so p'raps God will have mercy on me soon.'

John placed the little basket on his knees. 'I brought you something to eat and drink. I'm appointed master of the National School in Hope, Dick, and Mrs Bywater comes to help me in the house. She makes wonderful pies.' He opened the basket and placed the pie in the old man's hands. Dick broke off a small piece and put it in his mouth. Tears began to run down his cheeks. Then he choked as if the small fragment of pastry was too much for him to swallow. John quickly unstoppered the bottle of ale and passed it to him. Dick's tears flowed faster as he gulped some down. Then he ate and drank in silence until everything was gone.

'That's the first food I've had that tasted of summat since I come to this place.'

He licked his lips and pulled out an ancient handkerchief to wipe the crumbs away. Suddenly he became aware of the stubble on his chin.

'What must you think of me, with all this hair on my face, Master John. You know I always liked to have a good shave most days.'

'Do you find it hard to shave these days, Dick?'

'Not if I had the means. But we ain't allowed no razors in case we cuts our own throats. Wouldn't look good, would it, if we all did ourselves in, so they gives us all a shave 'bout once a week.'

Now it was John's turn for tears, but he did not want Dick to see them, so he stood up and turned away.

'I'm afraid I must go now, Dick. School opens on Monday and I have much to do.'

'I never got to school myself, 'cept a few weeks here and there. But 'tis different now. The young uns needs to 'ave the reading and figuring. I reckon you'll larn 'em well, Master John.'

'I shall try.'

'It was good of you to visit me, Master John.' Then after a brief pause he went on. 'Can I ask a favour of you?'

'Of course. What is it?'

'Would you have a look at my Annie's grave. See what needs doing, like.'

'Of course, I will, Dick. And put a few flowers there for you, yes?'

'I can't pay you for 'em, Master John. We ain't allowed to 'ave no money on us in 'ere.'

John had no reply. He took the old man's hand and shook it, then left before his sadness overwhelmed him.

Later that evening, John brought the log book into the schoolhouse. He carefully ruled off Miss Owen's last entry, so that he could begin his own, then he began to flick back through the pages, looking for some clue about his predecessor's disappearance. Suddenly, he remembered the letter the rector had given him, took it from his pocket, laid it on the blank page in the log book and read the following:

"The Reverend Whiting,
Correspondent to the Managers,
Hope Underhill National School
August 12th. 1879
Dear Sir,

I would ask you to inform the Managers that I must give up the post of Mistress at the above School with immediate effect. Circumstances have forced me to leave the village.

I hope you can find a suitable replacement as soon as possible.

Yours faithfully,
Harriet Owen"

Brief, matter-of-fact, and with no hint of what might have caused her sudden departure. The writer had given no forwarding address. The letter had been delivered to the rectory by hand and no one saw who delivered it.

John looked again at the letter and then turned back to the last entry Miss Owen had made in the school log book. One thing was obvious; the letter to the rector and the entry in the log had not been written by the same hand.

EIGHTEEN

Monday, 10th September 1879

On this day, I took up my duties as schoolmaster. Only thirty-two children in attendance, mainly due to work continuing in the fields. My assistant Agnes Beale, pupil-teacher, arrived early to discuss her duties. She has responsibility for the ten youngest pupils, but of those only seven were in school today. I must do all in my power to improve attendance. The behaviour of the pupils was generally good, but many were unable to concentrate on their tasks after the long break from studies.

The children seemed rather in awe of the new master. Perhaps because he was more than six feet in height, or perhaps they were cowed by the return of the cane to its hook on the side of the master's desk. John kept a stern demeanour on that first day, but he could feel nothing but pity for these children whose poverty was obvious from the state of their clothes. One of the oldest boys, poor Abel Downs, could hardly fit into his desk, and had long outgrown his clothes, his trousers ending well above his ankles and his jacket splitting down the back seam from straining to fit over his broadening shoulders. The girls for the most part were clean and tidy, though much effort had gone into darning old pinafores and lengthening last year's skirts. One of the youngest girls, named Hannah Green, had a terrible sore on her cheek, which she picked at most of the morning, so that it became red and angry by lunchtime.

When morning school ended, those children who did not go home for lunch hurried into the yard to be in the air and sun and the bigger boys became wild things. As John watched them run and leap and kick a half-deflated pig's bladder around the tiny yard, he remembered that all too soon they would be labouring in the fields from sunrise to sunset come rain, cold winds or even snow, just so that their parents could afford the rent for the damp, dark cottages they were crowded into. And those older girls, eleven or twelve years old, twirling around with their waist-long hair flying, would, in a few months' time be cleaning, polishing, scrubbing and scraping from the early hours till well into the evening, in the house of anyone who could afford to keep a servant.

By the end of the second week, the children had become used to their new master and he to them. As they slipped back into the school routine, John realised how well they had been taught by his predecessor. Most of them could cope with the work he set, so he was able to concentrate on those who found it difficult. Once or twice, he went beyond the curriculum and used his own experiences to enliven his geography lessons. He told the children about Africa, about the great Zambezi River and Victoria Falls. One afternoon, he began to tell them about David Livingstone. Not only did all the pupils listen attentively to him, but Miss Beale came to stand by the partition and listen to his story.

When the children had gone at the end of the day, Agnes came to him and asked, 'Mr Noble, tell me, are the people of Africa really black?'

'Yes, Agnes, though some are more of a dark brown, according to their tribe.'

'And this blackness remains even when they wash.'

'Yes, you see it is not a pigment applied to the skin but the skin itself that is black. It cannot be washed or rubbed away.'

'And the skin is black all over?'

John looked at this plain, pale, earnest young woman, who would go on to make a competent but unexciting teacher and tried to hide his blushes when he remembered the lust he had felt for some of those beautiful African women, especially after Elizabeth's miscarriages. He thought of the parts of their bodies that were not black, such as the palms of their hands and other more intimate places.

A few times each week it was necessary for John to give Agnes lessons, in preparation for her examinations the following June, but not once did the girl mention Miss Owen. At last John could contain himself no longer and asked, 'Did you like working with Miss Owen, Agnes?'

'Yes,' the girl replied coolly. 'She was very kind and clever and very pretty. But my father says she was a wicked woman and deserved to come to a bad end.'

John was so taken aback that he said nothing as Agnes left the room. Her father was a man who professed himself a committed Christian and took himself and his family off to Christian Fellowship meetings on the Welsh coast. After that, the schoolmaster and his assistant did not discuss Miss Owen again.

Since the term began, John had not had much time to think about Miss Owen's murder, but the following Saturday, he received a letter from Constable Oakes.

"Mr John Noble,

I am writing to tell you that the stranger as was mentioned by the gipsies has been traced to the port of Bristol, where it is known he took passage to America. It is said that he got the money for his passage by selling some articles of women's clothing and some small items of jewellery, so it seems most likely that he is our murderer. The police office has informed me that this being the most reasonable circumstance they have closed the case.

Yours truly,
Cedric Oakes,
Police Constable

PS. I hope you are successful in your new post."

John shook his head. He did not believe for one moment that the stranger from the gipsy camp had murdered Miss Owen, though he could see why Oakes might reach that conclusion. Much better to imagine that the murderer was someone with no connection to the village, except that brief stay with the gipsies, than to upset the apple cart with investigations nearer home.

Back at school, John carried out the daily dose of prayers and hymns without enthusiasm. He was expected to go through a set of readings from the scriptures, but he often replaced these by telling the familiar stories of Noah's ark, David and Goliath, or Moses in his own style, making them as dramatic as possible.

He also found punishment difficult to dispense, especially when the rudeness and inattention were, for the most part, not directed at him. The Reverend Whiting arrived each Friday morning to give religious instruction. He had managed to acquire a new housekeeper so his clothes were in better shape, but he looked older and more haggard week by week. The man had no idea how to deal with children. He saw them as inattentive, unruly savages and so, when he was with them, that was what they became. He would plough through the curriculum as if the children hardly existed, but he noted the worst behaviour in a little book, which he handed to John at the end of the morning, for him to punish the miscreants.

John's penalties were not severe, unless he really felt that punishment was justified. When a boy of eleven was caught bullying a younger, weaker child, he had no compunction in delivering several fierce strokes with the cane. And when the boy complained that Miss Owen had never used the cane John gave him three more strokes.

John's biggest disappointment was the continued poor attendance of his pupils. The numbers had risen slightly by the end of the third week, probably because the weather was worsening by mid-October, and there was less work in the fields, but it still wasn't as good as it should be. He had already written to several parents asking for an explanation of their children's absence, but the time had come to visit them in person.

NINETEEN

The weather had been dull for the last few weeks, mild enough but with constant low cloud, which made most days dark and depressing. But on the Friday afternoon of the fifth week the clouds dispersed and everyone's spirits lifted as the sun coloured the landscape again. At the end of the day, John chose a hymn the children liked, shortened his prayers, and let them go slightly early. Some of the older boys went whooping out as if they had been released from a life sentence, and some of the girls smiled as they wished him good afternoon. He had won over most of the children who attended the school; now he must bring the stray sheep into the fold.

He began with the most distant absentee, a girl of nine, who lived at Copse Farm Cottage, not far from that infamous barley field. Mrs Bywater had given John directions to the cottage and warned him that to get there, he must cross some fields belonging to the farmer who had quarrelled with Miss Owen about his son's attendance at school. In fact, the field where she had been murdered belonged to him. Mrs Bywater also told John that the mother of the absentee girl had been widowed a couple of years ago when her husband was killed in an accident on the farm.

'Nasty business it were. He was raking hay in the loft when part of the floor gave way. He fell onto his own pitchfork. It went right through him.'

Happy to be out of the schoolroom at the end of a long week, John strode up the hillside determined not to be depressed by thoughts of the murder, but strangely, he got the feeling that he was being followed. As he trod the path towards the cottage, which ran alongside a hedge of hazel and hawthorn, he sensed that someone was walking just behind him on the other side. Although the hedge had begun to lose some leaves, the mass of twigs and remaining greenery made it impossible to see through, and John could have sworn that a dark shape moved along with him. When he came to a gap in the hedge he laughed at his own foolishness. The field was full of cattle, and one of them was moving contentedly along the hedgerow, chewing clumps of tasty grass.

His path led to a stile in the corner of the field and as he climbed over, he saw the cottage directly ahead. Smoke rose up from its chimney into the still, clear sky. There might well be a frost tonight, thought John, the first of the season, and he was glad he had worn his thicker jacket.

The cottage was small but surrounded by a large, well-kept garden and an orchard with a few apples left among the dark fuzz of twigs at the tops of the trees. As John opened the wicket gate, a large brown dog lolloped towards him and he hesitated as it barked sharply, a few times. A woman called the dog off and it trotted away obediently, wagging its tail and whimpering softly, having accomplished what it had been trained to do, give warning of a visitor.

Mother and daughter stood near the open doorway of the cottage, which was still bathed in the evening light. Both were small and slim, with pale oval faces and straw-coloured hair. The older woman, though there did not seem that many years between them, wore her hair pinned up under a straw bonnet, while the girl's finer, lighter, locks flowed down beyond her waist. The dog lay collapsed at their feet, with its large head resting on its paws. The women said nothing but waited for John to introduce himself.

'Mrs Williams? And Miss Amy Williams?'

Both nodded but still said nothing. John removed his hat.

'My name is Noble. John Noble. I am the master at Hope Underhill School.'

Now that he was closer, he could see that the woman's clothes were clean but shabby and that the daughter had outgrown her dress, so that more of her thin, pale legs showed than was meant, and her feet were bare.

'Good evening, Mr Noble. I hope old Bodger didn't frighten you.'

'Not at all. He is obviously well trained.'

She looked straight at John with blue unblinking eyes. 'So, Mr Noble, master of the school at Hope. You have come to tell me that my Amy should be at school.

Amy, my dear, would you draw our visitor a glass of cider.'

'Oh no, you mustn't bother…' But the girl had gone.

'I've been expecting you, Mr Noble. You sent me a letter about my daughter's absence. I knew that if you were a proper schoolmaster, when I didn't reply, you'd come to find out why.'

John sensed no antagonism from the woman. Perhaps her modest smile even suggested some amusement. Amy returned with a glass of cider. It was not cloudy like some of the homemade stuff, but clear, golden and effervescent. He took a sip and it tasted very good, sharp for a moment, then sweet and satisfying. The evening seemed quite perfect. The sun warm on his neck, this neat little cottage set among its fruitful trees, this pretty woman… but no, he had his duty to do. He straightened his shoulders and tried to stand on his dignity.

'You see, I must make sure that all the pupils attend regularly, so that they can make progress, and earn the school its proper grant.'

'Won't you sit down, Mr Noble? Another glass?'

He would have loved to say yes, but it would not have been right. The woman sat on one of the simple upright chairs that had been brought out, so that they could enjoy the last rays of sun. She patted the seat of the other chair, took the empty glass from his hand and placed it on the bench beside the apple box. He sat down. Amy picked up the glass and went inside. John hoped she would not return with a refill. Mrs Williams spoke again.

'It was a terrible thing that happened to Miss Owen. My Amy thought the world of her.'

'So she attended regularly last year?'

'Yes… Oh don't worry, it's not because of you taking over. No, Amy likes school and I am sure she would get used to you.'

'Then what keeps her away?'

The woman shuddered slightly. The evening was becoming chill. She called to her daughter.

'Amy, would you bring me my shawl, please.'

The girl came out of the house with a ragged woollen shawl which she placed over her mother's shoulders. She stood for a moment beside her mother. They could be sisters, thought John.

'May I go in again, Mama. My feet are cold.'

'Then put on your boots.'

'Don't tease, Mama.' The girl blushed deeply. 'You know I have none.' Then she was gone.

'So, there you have it, Mr Noble. How can I send her to school without boots? Especially now that autumn is here.'

'I suppose that since your husband died you have found it hard—'

'Ah, someone has primed you well. Yes. People have been very kind. Farmer Hughes is letting me stay in the cottage, at least until next Michaelmas. Mrs

Hughes gives me employment whenever she can; cleaning, washing, helping in the dairy. And we can grow most of what we need. But it's the big things I can't find the money for, such as boots.'

'I think I might be able to help you there, Mrs Williams.'

Mrs Williams looked at him with a frank gaze.

'You see,' John lied. 'There is a fund, set up by the school managers, to help those in special need.' He quickly calculated what was left of his tiny legacy. 'It would be possible for me use that fund to cover the cost of boots for your daughter.'

There had never been the slightest bitterness in the woman's voice or any trace of self-pity. Now she smiled as if she had been granted a miracle.

'Oh, Mr Noble. Could you really do that? I would be so grateful. Amy is a clever girl and was doing well at school. I felt awful not being able to send her this term.'

John began to calculate how much a child's boots might cost and whether he had enough money on him now. He thought not. And anyway, he would not mind having an excuse to come back to this cottage. So, it was agreed that he should return early next morning with sufficient money for Mrs Williams and her daughter to get the weekly horse-drawn charabanc to the market in Churchtown and buy a pair of boots. Amy would be back at school on Monday.

John set off down the garden path with a sense of achievement. The sun had gone and the women were taking the apples indoors. Mrs Williams called out to him.

'Thank you again, John Noble. We will meet you at the end of the lane in the morning. My name is Ella, by the way.'

John raised his hat and climbed the stile. He felt warm in spite of the growing chill of the evening, and his heart was beating faster than his exercise required.

It was beginning to grow dark, so he took a short cut nearer to the farm. Before long, he had a feeling again of being watched, then he caught sight of someone near the hedge; a dark figure coming towards him. John stopped and prepared to defend himself, but as the figure came closer, he saw that it was just a lad of about twelve or thirteen.

'Are you Mr Noble, the new schoolmaster?' the boy asked.

'I am,' replied John. 'Have you been following me?'

'Yes.'

'And who are you?'

'Richard Hughes. From Copse Farm. I had to be sure who you were. Then I heard Mrs Williams call out your name. I have something for you.'

'Are you the boy Miss Owen wanted to stay on at school?'

'That's right. She got me learning right well. But I were needed on the farm. Especially since Mr Williams had his accident.'

'Well, what do you have for me?'

''Tis summat I found in the barley field when we fetched the reaping machine. She wore it all the time. Can you give it to him?'

'Him?'

'Aye, you'll know who when you opens it.'

John took a small brown paper package from the boy and unwrapped it to find a silver locket.'

'Were you watching me when I came to the field before? Was it you inside the wood?'

'Yes, I thought you was the new master, but I wasn't sure.'

'Would you have liked to stay on at school, Richard?'

'P'raps. But Dad needed me more.'

'Was your father angry with Miss Owen, Richard?'

'Aye. She kept on and on. But when she came to the farm and saw how things were, she understood and they parted friends. She could always do that. Make people like her, I mean. I canna understand nobody wanting her dead.'

'Well, Richard, I intend to find out who it was. And this,' he held up the locket, 'might just help me.'

Back at home, John lit a candle and lifted the locket carefully out of the paper. It was not expensive or

135

elaborate, but it was silver and it was well made. He pressed his fingernail into the groove at the side and the locket sprang open. As his eyes adjusted to the flickering candlelight he frowned in surprise. Inside was a photograph of a little boy, between three and four years old. He was the image of Harriet Owen.

TWENTY

Neither the raucous calls of the rooks, nor the church bell chiming six were needed to waken John next morning. He was more alert and eager to begin the day than he had been for a good while. There had been a slight frost overnight and the rising sun showed a sparkling world. The unheated bedroom made quick dressing a necessity and Mrs Bywater had not yet arrived to light the fires downstairs, so when he was dressed John put on his outdoor clothes and set off. He was better known in the village now, and the few villagers already about at that hour greeted him more warmly.

It was far too early to meet Ella Williams and her daughter so John set off in the opposite direction towards the Devil's Peak. It was strange how different the hills were on either side of the valley. Long Hill to the east was smooth, rounded and mostly green where sheep and ponies clipped the grass, but Devil's Peak on the other side was topped with a series of rocky outcrops, breaking through the bracken and heather like the vertebrae of a mythical monster. In the day, these natural cairns were just heaps of rock inviting the walker to climb to the top and look westward to the clustered mountains of North Wales. But when the sun set behind them, or mist half concealed them, they would appear as dark and forbidding as ancient fortresses. Beyond this ridge of weathered rock were the mines where lead ore had been gouged from the earth since Roman times.

John would not have time to climb to the rocky summit this morning, but he could make the halfway point where a group of pines stood on a ledge overlooking the village. The slope was steep. Soon he was warm from his exertions and his breath turned to steam as it puffed from his nostrils into the chill air. He had just turned off the road and onto the track that led up the hill when he saw someone standing on the ledge among the trees. The man was behaving in a peculiar manner and John instinctively drew back behind a hawthorn bush so as not to embarrass him. The man began to cry aloud, and as John peeped through the bush, he saw that it was the Reverend Whiting. The rector fell to his knees, lifting his hands in prayer then bringing them down to the ground and moaning his incantation. John was reminded of the witch doctors in Africa, cursing someone from another tribe, or trying to drive disease from one of their own.

The rector had slowly been sinking into an unhealthy mental state for some time. His visits to the school to give religious instruction had become shorter each time and the previous week he had not appeared at all. His Sunday sermons, which John felt obliged to hear, had become meaningless rambles and the rector often seemed to forget where he was, his bloodshot eyes staring wildly into space. Now, it seemed, he had reached a crisis. As John slipped away the rector cried out, 'Oh God! Oh God!'

TWENTY-ONE

John had agreed to meet Ella at eight o'clock, where the farm lane met the road from Hope Underhill to Churchtown. There was no need for haste and he had the money for the boots in his pocket, so he turned into Back Lane which curled around the village and met the road to Churchtown at the other end.

The cottages here were small and primitive, not much more than hovels. In them lived the poorest people of the village, with the largest families, sharing a single hand pump for their drinking water and a greasy looking stream for all their other watery needs. Whether thatched or slated, most of the roofs needed repair and hardly a window remained entirely intact. These cottages usually consisted of a living room and kitchen downstairs and only one or at the most two bedrooms above, so as the day warmed up the inhabitants would gladly spill out from the damp and foetid rooms into the outdoors. The men would work if they could find it, the women would sweep and shake out the detritus of crowded living and the children, if not at school, would mind the babies or play some simple games when they could get away.

Halfway along the lane John met a trio of his pupils, who had managed to escape from family duties and were setting off for a day's fishing, with some homemade, and probably useless, tackle. They were laughing and chattering happily until they saw their schoolmaster, when they fell silent and passed by in single file on the other side of the lane. John hated having that effect on them. He gave them a polite greeting and the boys mumbled one in return as they hurried past. How would they have greeted Miss Owen he wondered? Oh, well, he thought, I have only been at the school a few weeks and they are not altogether used to me yet.

As he strode steadily along, John wondered about Ella. Had he been fooled by the evening light, the fecund orchard, even perhaps by that splendid cider? Would she seem, in the full light of day, more ordinary and less attractive? Then he saw her, those blonde curls tucked up neatly under her best bonnet and her scrubbed face shining in the morning sun. She wore her best dress, which was probably quite old, but from this distance looked well enough and fitted her fine figure snugly. She and Amy were sitting on a large sack on top of a farm wagon. Next to them was a pen full of sheep and beside the horses stamping impatiently between the shafts, stood a large man holding the reins. John was disappointed. He had hoped for a few minutes alone with Ella before the horse-drawn charabanc arrived.

Ella smiled and gave a little wave; John sensed that, perhaps, she shared his disappointment.

The driver made fast the reins and approached John, holding out his hand.

'Edward Hughes.' He shook John's hand with a powerful grip. 'I knew your father well. I remember you an' all as a young'n. Natural like on adjoining farms.'

Now John remembered him, though the man had put on a deal of weight and his frizzy mop of hair had turned grey.

'I met the ladies walking down the lane and as I'm off to Churchtown myself I offered them a lift. Mrs Williams explained about the boots. I consider that a right noble gesture.'

Then he saw the unintended pun and laughed aloud. John liked Hughes at once. Suddenly, he took John's arm, drew him a little away from the cart and became serious.

'It was a terrible thing that happened to Miss Owen. I can hardly believe it still. Of course, we didn't allus see eye to eye, as you've probably 'eard. But thank God, we parted friends. She were a wonderful teacher. Made my lad a right good scholar. And pretty as a picture. That were a wicked thing that was done to 'er. An' in one of my fields an' all.'

Farmer Hughes was one of those men whose face clearly showed their feelings. His thoughts of the last mistress and her doom had drawn down his mouth at the edges. Then his face lifted and his smile returned.

'I have 'eard you'm doing well at the school yourself. Young Amy Williams will be a good addition to your flock. Bright and 'andsome like the mother. Her father were a good-looking man an' all but a bit late in the queue when they were dishing out brains.'

He crossed the road and leaned on the wooden gate. John joined him.

'You mean...'

'Aye, bit like, accident prone 'e were. Before the last one finished him off he were always injuring himself one way or 'nother. 'Tis said that's why young Amy never 'ad no younger brothers or sisters, but that's just idle gossip and I should be damned for spreading it.'

Mr Hughes cleared his throat, spat into the field and pointed.

'See down there? That's where my land joined your father's. I wanted to take it over when he left, but squire wouldn't 'ave it. Dinna want none of his tenants getting too big for 'is boots, I suppose. Squire were all right when he were younger, till his wife left him. Now, he's worse than useless as a landlord. Tell him the hunt has ruined your fences, he'll say, "Ah, but they got the damned fox dain't they?" But quick enough to interfere when he's a mind. Like young Ella's cottage. I don't need it now my lad's joined me on the farm. But a few months back, squire sends that son of his round to tell me I must send her packing. I wunna do it, leastways, not till next autumn and perhaps by then...'

He gave John a strange look and continued in a conspiratorial tone.

'I'll tell you summat else an' all. I wouldn't trust that Robert Moreton where any woman was concerned. When I went down to the school to have it out with Miss Owen about my lad staying on at school, I heard them quarrelling, Miss Owen and Moreton. He come bursting out, breathing fire like, and stormed away, leaving the door open. I peeped in and saw her sitting at her desk, 'er head on her arms, sobbin' away. So, I just left her and come 'ome.'

There was a pause while he remembered the scene and John pondered its implications, then the farmer's face became business-like again.

'Well, 'tis time to get on, or my sheep wunt get sold and no boots'll get bought. Good to meet you, Master Noble. Or Schoolmaster Noble I should say. Good luck to you with that lot down at the school. It won't be easy for you with that lunatic rector on your back all the time.' The farmer's mood changed again as he spoke vehemently. 'I'm not a man of hate, Mr Noble. Most men I like and the rest I can tolerate, but not him.'

Hughes turned away. For a big man, he was very agile. He grabbed the reins and leapt up onto the cart, which jerked forward. John quickly handed Ella the money for the boots. The ladies wobbled on their sack and held on to one another, giggling as the cart moved off. Then Ella smiled again and shouted, 'I'll be bringing Amy to school on Monday, Mr Noble.' John smiled back and waved. At least they would meet again quite soon. However, it was not of Ella that John was thinking as he walked back to the village, but of Robert Moreton and Miss Owen. What was that all about? That quarrel! Those tears! It was time, John thought, to speak to Robert Moreton. He would strike while the iron was hot and go to the manor this afternoon.

TWENTY-TWO

The years had not been kind to Sir Digby Moreton. He was in his late sixties but looked much older, once very tall, but stooping now, his jowls drooping like an old hound. His hair was long, thin and completely white. When a manservant brought him into the room, John was not sure whether the old man could see him, but as soon as they were alone Sir Digby said, 'You're very like your father, you know.'

'So I am told, Sir Digby.'

'Fine man, your father. Sorry to hear he has passed on. Do sit down, young man.'

John looked round the room. It was a fine, regency style drawing room, but now quite dilapidated, with wallpaper long faded and dusty curtains that looked as if one tug would rip them apart. The crowded furniture was unpolished, thick with dust and piled up with clothes, papers, sporting equipment and dogs. There were small dogs lying on the chairs, middle sized dogs stretched out on the settee, and large dogs on the floor. Sir Digby lifted a stick and pushed one of the dogs off a chair to make room for John. Hairs and dust rose in a cloud. The room stank.

Sir Digby sat back in his chair with his eyes closed. John wondered if he had gone to sleep. One foot in the grave, he thought. Yet Sir Digby still rode and even hunted once or twice during the season. Put him in the saddle, they said, and the years fell away from him. Suddenly, the old man's red rimmed eyes flickered open like a lizard's.

'So, you are master of the school. Is it going well? I am still officially one of the managers, but I find it hard to get to meetings these days, and if I do go, I generally fall asleep. Mind you, I still try to keep informed.'

Another pause. His eyes closed and opened again.

'Terrible thing that happened to that young woman. Terrible! And she was such a beauty. But by all accounts, she was playing with fire. I believe you came to see my son.'

'Yes, Sir Digby.'

'Gone abroad. Usually goes about this time of year. Likes the sun you know. And the casinos. You must be about the same age as Robert. I remember Maria visiting your mother as soon as she was over her own confinement.'

The squire had been nearly forty when he went off to London and came back with a wife. She was half Italian, they said, with striking dark looks. Where she had come from no one knew. Some thought she might have been an actress or a singer. She certainly had a strong voice and could be heard half a mile away cursing a horse, a servant or Sir Digby himself. For a short while she tried to play the lady of the manor, learning to ride and hunt and shoot, visiting and bestowing largesse upon the tenants. Then she bore Sir Digby a child. After that, she seemed to tire of the whole thing and when Robert was about four years old, she ran off with an officer from a regiment that was using Long Hill for manoeuvres before embarking for the Crimea. She was never heard of again.

The squire never divorced her, perhaps hoping that one day she would return. He hardly ever looked at another woman, or so John's parents had said. In fact, the whole village was rife with gossip about the squire and his son. Robert was denied nothing. There were no boundaries. He was allowed whatever he wanted. Servants were abused. Governesses left in tears. He was sent home from school, for bullying other boys and stealing from the masters. When he went to another school, he was soon sent home again.

In his early twenties, Robert joined the army and showed great courage in battle. He was tall, handsome and at that age slim and athletic. His father supplied him with a generous allowance, and women gave him whatever he wanted. But as he grew older his looks began to fade. He put on weight and his skin began to coarsen with gorging on too much food and drink. He caught diseases from his constant need for sexual pleasure, and his temper seemed to worsen. Then there was a scandal involving another officer. The man died of his wounds and Robert was dishonourably discharged.

So, he returned home and rampaged around the district. There were rumours of illegitimate children fathered up and down the valley; there were quarrels resulting in legal battles over unpaid debts. There were accusations of physical assault and there were numerous occasions when servants were sent out to find him and bring him home, senseless with drink.

The squire had been silent for a while. Now he spoke confidentially to John.

'Sometimes, I worry about my son. He doesn't seem to want to settle down. Not like you, eh? Perhaps when I've gone and he's got the estate to worry about...'

John felt that the time had come to ask some questions.

'You mentioned my predecessor earlier, Sir Digby. I wonder... did your son know Miss Owen?'

The squire's attitude changed abruptly.

'What d'you mean? Know her?'

'I heard that they had quarrelled.'

'Did you, by Jove! Well, I think you would do better than to listen to village gossip.'

The squire grabbed the stick that lay beside him and struggled to his feet. John stood too. When the squire straightened his back, they were face to face.

'Whether my son knew that young woman or not, is no business of yours, young man. I think you've overstretched your welcome. I'd like you to leave, immediately. And I'd advise you to stop meddling. As far as that young woman is concerned, the culprit has been found and the police have closed the case.'

The squire hobbled across to the fireplace and pulled a rope on the wall beside it. Within seconds that same elderly manservant reappeared.

'Stebbings. Show this young man out. And if he should return at any time he must not be admitted.'

'Very well, Sir Digby.'

John said no more but followed the servant out to the hallway. As Stebbings opened the door, he smiled at John and whispered, 'Touched a raw nerve there I reckon. You mustn't mind the old man, sir. And if you were wanting to speak to young Robert, I believe he may be back soon, for more money.'

TWENTY-THREE

The weather on Monday morning was dreadful, heavy rain pushed by a strong westerly wind. Consequently, attendance at school was low and by the time the bell stopped ringing only twenty-four children had arrived, including three infants, and no Amy Williams. John was disappointed. He had hoped to see Ella, however briefly, and he felt let down because she had promised to bring Amy.

Two more pupils arrived during prayers. He made them stand at the door and shake off as much of the rain as they could. As usual most of the children were inadequately dressed and, therefore, wet through. Now, they must sit in their damp clothes all day. But at least the stove was lit and drawing well. As the day progressed the children sitting nearest the fire would begin to steam, and the smell would not be sweet.

Prayers were over and the pupils had begun the reading lesson when there was a timid knock on the classroom door. John called out, 'Come in,' and the door opened to reveal Ella, who beckoned John to come to the door. She was very wet and flushed.

'I'm sorry we're late, Mr Noble, but the rain was so bad we had to shelter a couple of times, and Amy's new boots, being wet, began to pinch her feet. Do forgive us.'

John ushered Amy into the classroom, showing her a vacant desk near the front. When he turned back to Ella and met her sky-blue gaze he would have forgiven her anything. He felt a warm flush reaching his cheeks and was glad that the children's attention was on Amy returning to her place in class.

'Thank you, Mr Noble. I will collect Amy this evening. But from tomorrow she must make her own way to school.'

John would have liked to go on gazing into those azure eyes, but Ella gave him a quick smile and left. He returned to his desk, handed one of the readers to Amy and the lesson continued.

It had been a pleasant surprise for John to find a set of interesting and appropriate readers in a cupboard. So often in his previous schools the books were difficult or dull or both. He remembered one particular set aimed at Standard IV that included the following sentence: "This property in gold of being capable of extension to so extraordinary a degree is owing to its great tenacity or cohesion of particles." Such a text would send most of his pupils to sleep in minutes. He had asked the rector where these more suitable books had come from and was informed that Miss Owen had thrown out most of the readers soon after she arrived and persuaded the managers to find the funds for new ones. The rector gave a wry smile, and said that once the managers had met Miss Owen, they found it difficult to refuse her anything.

When it was Amy's turn to read, she did so accurately and in a lively manner. John found it difficult to concentrate that morning because every time he glanced at Amy he was reminded of Ella. Some of the older boys kept glancing towards Amy, who had removed her wet bonnet and let down her long golden hair.

When morning break came it was still raining, so the children had to remain in the classroom. At first, John sensed antagonism towards Amy amongst some of the older girls, but her natural friendliness soon won them over, and by the end of the day it was if she had never been absent.

The rain ceased in the early afternoon and by the time the school day ended small clouds were scudding across the clearing sky. As the children hurried out of school Amy gave her mother a quick hug and nodded when Ella asked if her first day had gone well, then she joined two of her classmates who were skipping in the small yard.

Most parents did not collect their children from school. Sometimes, older brothers and sisters came for the youngest ones, but generally children came to school and went home again on their own from a very early age.

John was concerned about Amy walking such a long way home.

'No need to worry, Mr Noble. The Chapman sisters walk nearly as far.' She indicated the girls now swinging the rope for Amy to skip. 'She'll be with them to the end of the lane. And when I can I'll meet her there.'

'But it will be dark before she gets home. And there has been a murder quite near to your cottage.'

'But that's been solved, hasn't it? The murderer was found. And surely, you'll be cutting the lunchtime soon and sending the children home at half past three. That's what Miss Owen did. Anyway, us country girls can see in the dark, Mr Noble. Didn't they teach you that at college?'

John was happy to be teased by this delightful woman, but at that moment, Amy called to her mother.

'I'm going on with Doris and Elsie, Ma. You can catch us up.'

'Well, I must go too, Mr Noble. Oh, I s'pose you'll be at the harvest feast? Mrs Hughes has asked me to help.'

'I believe it is expected of me, Mrs Williams.'

'Don't force yourself just for our benefit, Mr Noble.'

'Oh, I didn't mean....'

But Ella laughed and ran to catch up with the others.

When John closed the school and stepped back into the house he found Mrs Bywater in the kitchen ironing his

154

shirts. The flat irons were lined up on the range, so that as one cooled she put it back and transferred her cloth to the handle of another. Her sleeves were rolled up and her head was uncovered but even so she was sweating a little in the hot kitchen. John remembered that he had not yet shown her Miss Owen's locket, so he went into the living room, took it from the little drawer and called to Mrs Bywater.

'Can you come in here for a moment, Mrs B? I have something to show you.'

As soon as Mrs Bywater saw the locket she exclaimed, 'Why that's it, Mr Noble! That's Harriet's little locket. Wherever did you find it?'

'I didn't find it, Mrs B. But the one who did, asked me to return it to the person pictured inside. Did you ever see inside it yourself?'

'No, but I noticed that whenever poor dear Harriet opened it her face would grow sad, and once or twice I thought her eyes might be brimming with tears. So, who is it pictured within?'

'Here,' John said, passing the locket to Mrs B. 'See for yourself.'

She opened the locket and took it over to the light.

'Good gracious! Who can he be? He looks so much like her.'

'A much younger brother perhaps? Or a nephew? Whoever it is his initial is G. At least, that's what written on the back of the photograph.'

Suddenly John sniffed. 'What's that smell, Mrs B? Something burning?'

The woman ran to the kitchen, calling out, 'Damn and…'

When she returned, her face was red with embarrassment as she held up a smouldering shirt with an iron shaped hole in its back.

'Oh, Mr Noble, what will you think of me? My language. But when you called me in here, I forgot…'

John laughed. 'Never mind, Mrs B. At least it's in the back. If I keep my jacket on, no one will know.'

Mrs B. clasped her hand over her mouth and muttered, 'Oh no!'

'Really, Mrs B! It's not the end of the world.'

'No, it's not this. I've just remembered something.'

'Something about Miss Owen?'

The woman nodded.

'Come and sit down and tell me.'

Mrs Bywater sat down, gazed again at the open locket and began her tale.

TWENTY-FOUR

'It were last Christmas. The very last day of term. Miss Owen had arranged a little concert, for after school ended. The parents and the managers were invited. Just a few songs and recitations. And a carol or two, for all to sing. Harriet played the piano very well. The children had been practising for weeks. It was lovely really. Even the squire came. His son brought him; that was a surprise. But he wouldn't go into the concert, not Robert Moreton. Sat in here, listening through the open door and drinking from a silver flask. Every so often, he'd get up and peek through the door, but it weren't the children he were gawping at, I can tell you that.

'Anyway, the concert was almost over when there was a knock at the door. It was a telegram for Miss Owen. When the song ended, I took it to her in case there was an answer. As she read the telegram, she turned quite pale. I thought for a minute she were going to faint. She took a glass of water from the top of the piano and drained it. She told me that there was no answer, then went over to the rector, who was sat beaming at her, the silly old fool. I went back into the house and told the telegram boy there was no answer.

'Soon after, Harriet rushed in saying that someone in her family was very ill and that she must leave at once. She hoped to catch the last up-train from Churchtown at half past seven. It was then that Robert Moreton spoke up, saying she need not rush as he would take her to the station in the gig, and arrange for someone else to take his father home. I weren't too happy about that. Robert Moreton has a reputation with the women as you've probably heard. The thought of him alone with Harriet on that dark evening worried me. Yet I reckoned she could look after herself. Anyway, Harriet thanked him, and hurried upstairs to pack. In her haste, she dropped the telegram and its envelope. I heard the rector next door, thanking Miss Owen for arranging the concert and then leading the audience in a prayer.

'I went towards the kitchen to make up a cold meat sandwich for Harriet to take on her journey. As I left the room I glanced back and saw Robert Moreton pick up the telegram and place it on the mantelpiece.

'The concert ended and the guests left, and when I came back in here there was just the rector, Robert Moreton and Harriet, who was putting on her cloak. I gave her the little meal and she threw her arms around me.

'"Oh, Mrs B. You are wonderful. I do hope you have a splendid Christmas. And you, Rector. I shall let you know when I can return."

'She picked up a small travelling case and followed the squire's son out into the night. The members of the audience were filtering out. The rector wished me good night and left as well.

'Next day, I came in here to tidy up and saw that the telegram was still on the mantelpiece, but the envelope was missing. I thought little of it at the time. But I'm ashamed to say that curiosity got the better of me so, before I scrumpled it up, and threw it in the grate, I read it.'

'Well, what did it say?' asked John.

'G very ill. Stop. Come at once!'

TWENTY-FIVE

That year the harvest feast at Copse Farm was the latest it had been in living memory. The weather had continued to be changeable since the barley had been cut in early September, so some stooks had to be left to dry in the few fine days before being carried by wagon to the rickyard.

Sometime soon the contractors would arrive, their lumbering traction engines pulling huge wooden threshing boxes swaying and bumping up the narrow lane to the farm. These would be set up near the rough ricks and the drivebelts attached from the traction engines to the wheels on the threshing machines. Then the soft thump, thump of the huge pistons on the traction engines would quicken and the gleaming flywheels would spin while the sheaves were fed into the machines.

The crop would be separated into grain which flowed into the sacks at the back of the machine, and straw which would be built into a rick the size of a barn and thatched neatly to keep it dry through the winter. Farmer Hughes hoped that it could all be accomplished before winter began in earnest, so that his men would not have to work on the exposed rick or straddle the threshing machine with the frost biting into their limbs. The work was dangerous at the best of times, but numb wrists and stinging feet sometimes led to carelessness and a tumble into that rattling machinery could be fatal.

'Well,' said Farmer Hughes, 'at least we've got a bit of a crop this year. Not like that poor one last year.' He would show his gratitude by making this the best feast there had ever been.

There were some cynics, usually those not invited to the feast, who said that the farmers used these feasts to make up for the poor wages and harsh conditions forced on their labourers all year round. Indeed, wages were poor and working hours very long, especially for the lads of twelve and thirteen, who were expected to keep up with the grown men, but when it came to the feast there was no holding back.

For more than a week, the farmer's wife, daughters, and anyone else who could be roped in would be cooking from dawn to dusk, and the tables set up in the barn would groan with roasts, pies and puddings of every kind. Eighteen-gallon casks of cider were tapped and, usually, emptied by the end of the day.

Ella had been working alongside Mrs Hughes for several days. She was an accomplished cook and Mrs Hughes left some of the more complicated dishes entirely in her charge. She loved to watch Ella as she worked, her fine figure moving elegantly among the others, her golden hair catching the light and those large blue eyes smiling at everyone. Sometimes, when Mrs

Hughes compared her own daughter's plainness with Ella's good looks, she was slightly envious, but she liked Ella and pitied her misfortune. She hoped that those looks might attract another husband before they faded. Indeed, as her husband whispered to her when John arrived, 'Now there's someone who might do very well, being a widower himself.'

Ella enjoyed the camaraderie and sense of excitement in the build up to the feast. Nevertheless, she was glad that Amy had returned to school. Ella had been a quick learner in the few years she had attended school and she had often dreamed of getting away from the village and doing something other than going into service. But her parents were struggling with a large family, so as soon as she was twelve years old, she had been sent to work at the doctor's house on the other side of the valley.

She hated her new life. The hours were long, up at six in the morning and never finished much before nine at night. Her only free time was on Sunday morning, so that she could go to church, but Ella would run all the way home to spend a few hours with her family instead. The time would speed by and then she would have to return to her lonely attic room, put on her maid's uniform and present herself to the dour Mrs McKenzie, the doctor's wife.

Little surprise then when Ella, aged seventeen, met and married Alec Williams, a good-looking lad of nineteen who was helping with the hay in the doctor's meadow. When Alec got the job of general labourer at Copse Farm they moved into the cottage and Ella was merely eighteen when Amy was born. But it was just after Amy's christening that things began to go wrong. Alec started to have headaches, not too often, but very severe. He would grow pale and his handsome features would contort with the pain. Over the next few years, the headaches became more frequent and more intense, making it difficult to concentrate on his work. Then the first accident occurred.

Alec was a ploughman by this time, and one day, as he was unhitching one of the big plough horses, a particularly bad headache struck and he dropped the chains which got tangled up with the horse's hooves. The horse lashed out to free itself and its huge metal-clad hoof caught Alec square between the legs. He lay in the damp furrows in terrible pain for a couple of hours until Ella came with his midday meal. She took a sack off the horse's back, sat Amy on it next to Alec, told her not to move and ran for help.

Alec was carried, moaning in agony, back to the cottage. The doctor came to look at the vicious bruising and gave some ointment to Ella which would ease the pain, but nothing else could be done. The bruises faded and the pain went, but after that Alec was unable to make love. Ella never complained though she often longed to feel him inside her again and she regretted that Amy was destined to be an only child.

Amy was seven years old when the second accident occurred. The headaches had become less frequent and Alec had been promoted to foreman. He was a fine man to look at, his face still handsome, his body slim but strong, and he was an excellent foreman, always leading by example and working harder than any of his men. Perhaps that was his downfall.

They were moving hay up into the loft, next to the byre, so that it could be dropped through the chutes into the feeding troughs for the cattle below. Alec carried more hay on his pitchfork and moved faster than anyone else. He moved around the upper floor with confidence and grace, seeming to know exactly where the half floor ended, even when it was hidden by hay. He was standing right on the edge when a headache came upon him, blinding and excruciating. He dropped the fork which fell handle first to the floor below and stood for a moment, its spikes in the air, humming. In his blindness, Alec slipped off the edge and fell straight onto the spikes which went right through his chest and killed him instantly.

TWENTY-SIX

On Friday afternoon, John closed the school and walked with Amy up to Copse Farm to share the harvest feast. He was not sure why he had been invited, after all he had not contributed in any way to the harvest, but he was greeted heartily by Farmer Hughes as he shook John's hand. Amy, who had hardly spoken during their walk, ran across to her mother who looked up briefly at John and smiled, rather wanly he thought, but perhaps that was because she was so busy. The other guests were arriving and there was much to do. Even Amy was soon employed carrying dishes to the table.

John was placed between Mr Hughes' daughters. Margaret on his right, in her late teens, reminded him of his wife Elizabeth when they had first met, that same plumpish plainness offset by youth and health. On his other side simpered Mary, fifteen or so, squat and shy. The conversation soon turned to education and John discovered that both girls had been sent to a day school in Churchtown run by a refined spinster called Miss Wimpole. It was obvious that Farmer Hughes had ambitions for his daughters. His son was away looking after the sheep.

At last, after a brief speech by Farmer Hughes, the feast began. John had not eaten since breakfast so the food was welcome and the drink gave him the courage to talk more openly to the girls sitting beside him. They were soon engrossed in his tales of Africa, their eyes growing wider with wonder by the moment. John kept glancing at Ella as she moved around the table, filling jugs and bringing fresh bread, but the few times that she returned his gaze it was with less than her usual friendliness. At last, she came to his part of the table and as she leaned over to reach a jug, she whispered, 'Mr Noble, I would be glad of a word with you later on.'

As she moved on again Mrs Hughes called to her, 'Now then, Ella lass, you'm done enough. Sit yourself down and get summat t' eat.' So, Ella made her way to the end of the long table and sat among the working men, who were delighted to make room for her.

The table began to reappear as empty plates and dishes were taken away by a contingent of the workers' wives. Three musicians had arrived during the feast and were tuning up their instruments, a fiddle, a flute and a concertina. Farmer Hughes went into a huddle with the musicians and after a few chords from them he began to sing in a confident baritone.

There were three men come out from the west,
The victory to try,
And these men made a solemn vow,
John Barleycorn should die.

It was a song John had heard dozens of times before at harvest time. The words varied slightly according to where the singers came from, but he was always moved by them, especially when everyone joined in to tell the story of the farming cycle.

They ploughed, they sowed, they harrowed him in,
Throwed clods all on his head'
And these three men rejoicing went,
John Barleycorn was dead.

Soon, everyone was singing the universal story of seedtime and harvest, death and rebirth.

The sun shone warm and the wind blew soft
And it rained for a day or so.
John Barleycorn felt the wind and rain
And he began to grow.

So, they hired men with sharpest scythes
To cut him off at the knee;
And worst of all John Barleycorn
They served him barbarously.

For a moment, John was back in that barley field barely a month ago, watching the reaping machine moving through the barley crop, felling the stalks, until the knives got caught in that poor woman's dress. He shuddered at the memory. Harriet Owen had been cut down cruelly like John Barleycorn but her seed had died with her.

The story continued. John Barleycorn was tied up, taken to the barn, beaten until the seed was shaken from the stalks, dried in the kiln, crushed between the miller's stones and mashed in the tub. Then fiddle, flute and squeezebox rose to a crescendo and all the voices roared as the story came back to the feast.

So, put your wine in your finest glass,
Your cider in a pewter can,
Put John Barleycorn in the old brown jug,
For he's proved the strongest man.

At the end of the song a cheer went up, followed by silence as everyone drank deep from whatever glass, pot or jug they had in hand. Then the tables and benches were removed and the dancing began. The Hughes girls claimed John first and he danced with each in turn for a while. Both were short for their ages and as he twirled them round, they gazed up at him, laughing happily. Ella had disappeared.

At last, John excused himself, saying that he was thirsty, and made his way into the kitchen, which was full of women scraping the debris from bowls and plates and stacking them in the huge sink. They hardly noticed John as he filled a mug and looked around. Ella was standing near the open door, and as soon as she saw him she slipped outside. He put down the mug, wiped his brow, crossed to the door, saying, 'Time for some fresh air,' and went out.

It had grown so dark, that at first he could not see Ella standing under the large oak that filled the yard. Then she called out softly, 'John! Over here!'

His heart leapt at the sound of her voice using his first name, as he went to join her. Soon, his eyes adjusted to the darkness and he could make out her pale face. He came as close to her as he dared and whispered, 'What is it, Ella? What is worrying you?'

'I'm surprised you noticed. You a guest of honour and me just a serving wench. You were so busy chattering and dancing with Miss Mary and Miss Margaret I thought you would never come to find me.'

Was she teasing him again, or was she just a little jealous? Either way he was happy in her company. He would have liked to lean a little closer and place a kiss on her pale cheek, but instead he asked, 'You had something to tell me?'

'Yes. Robert Moreton is back. I've had a visit from him. It's not the first time he's been to my cottage. Soon after Alec was killed he came a-visiting. Pretended it were sympathy. Asked if he could help me in any way. But I know just the sort of man he is. He began to visit regular like and was full of flattery and pretended kindness. Then one night he tried to… but thank God, Amy came into the room just in time. And not long after that *she* arrived in the village.'

'She?'

'Miss Owen. He stopped pestering me and tried to get me out of the cottage instead, out of spite I suppose. But Mr Hughes weren't having that.'

'He's a good man.'

'Aye, he is.'

'So, you think Robert Moreton started pestering Miss Owen instead?'

'It's more than likely. But he kept it very quiet.'

'I suspected there was something between them. That's why I tried to speak to him.'

'Aye, and that's why he came to see me. He seems to think that you and I have become friends.'

'I hope we have.'

Ella was quiet for a moment, then said, 'He told me to warn you. To stop asking questions, to keep away from the manor, and to keep away from him.'

'Well, that pretty much confirms that he has something to hide. There's no way I'm going to leave him alone now.'

'No, John. Let it be. Harriet is dead. What good can it do? And Robert Moreton is a dangerous man.'

'Aye, perhaps more dangerous than anyone imagines. And now that Miss Owen is dead, he might turn his attentions elsewhere again.'

Ella gasped, 'Oh no, I hadn't thought…'

John felt for Ella's hand and gently squeezed it.

'Well, Mrs Williams, you have given me the message. Now, I suggest that we return to the feast and forget Robert Moreton for a while. Do you like to dance?'

It was well after midnight when John returned to the schoolhouse. He was weary from dancing, a little drunk, and very happy indeed. He remembered Farmer Hughes' words when John went to give thanks and say goodbye.

'Well, lad, I likes to make people happy. And I reckon I've done that for at least two young people tonight.'

But a sudden thought brought John down to Earth. He remembered that there was to be a managers' meeting next day, the first since his appointment, and that the managers would want to see the school log.

'Damn,' he muttered. He had been much too busy this week to complete it. Never mind. He would get up early in the morning and do it, but then he thought that this would be unlikely after such an evening of festivities. Better do it tonight.

John lit a lamp and made his way, rather unsteadily, into the schoolroom. He wondered if anyone passing by might see the lamp and think the ghost of his predecessor had come back to haunt the school. He opened the desk and found the log. He prepared pen and ink and wrote a few bland sentences for the week, then tried to work out the average attendance, but the numbers whirled round in his head and his eyes kept closing. At last, he entered what seemed a likely average, and went to close the big black book, but in his weary state he knocked it to the floor. When he bent to pick it up, he noticed a tiny piece of paper on the floor that must have been tucked inside the log book.

He turned up the lamp and studied the fragment of paper torn, apparently, from the corner of a letter, and having written on it in small, neat copperplate the following address.

29 Trafalgar Place,
Blackington,
Lancashire.

John placed the scrap of paper in the drawer with the rest of Miss Owen's things, for he was sure it had some connection with her, climbed wearily up the stairs, removed his boots and dropped onto the bed, still dressed, and fell fast asleep.

TWENTY-SEVEN

It was over a week since John had found the little slip of paper with that Lancashire address. The managers' meeting had gone smoothly enough and they were happy for the new master to continue in his post. In the days that followed, John consulted maps and studied his Bradshaw in preparation for making the journey to Lancashire as soon as he could. On Friday, the rector came to give religious instruction as usual, but offered no explanation or apology for his previous absence. He seemed calmer than of late, but very quiet. Perhaps, thought John, he is getting over Miss Owen's death at last.

The Reverend Whiting informed John that the school would be closed on the following Monday and Tuesday for a brief half term holiday, but otherwise hardly spoke. John didn't mention the piece of paper he had found but realised that the short holiday would give him the opportunity to locate the address and find out who lived there.

He must go into Shrewsbury on the Saturday to collect the shirts he had ordered, which were now sorely needed. On the Sunday he had promised to visit Dick in the workhouse and he knew the misery it would cause the old man if he did not go. So, he would travel to Lancashire on the Monday.

John had not seen Ella since the harvest feast but Amy had attended school each day, so when school ended on Friday, he gave her a note for Ella, explaining about the address and that he was going to find it. He had hoped to see them both at church on Sunday morning, but they did not appear.

Now John was on his way to Lancashire. His small travelling case contained a change of clothing and the few items belonging to Miss Owen, including that locket, which he had wrapped carefully in a clean handkerchief.

The train seemed to fly across the flat green pastureland of north Shropshire, with its neat farms and fields crowded with herds of fat cattle. This was one of the more prosperous farming districts renowned for its butter and cheese. John knew the line to Nantwich well, for it was the one he had taken to and from school for many years. Beyond that, he was travelling into a part of England as foreign to him as Africa had been less than a decade ago.

John changed trains at Crewe and was soon in Manchester, where he took another train to Rochdale, a vast man-made conurbation, spreading across the green skin of the countryside like a large red sore. The sky above was darkened not with clouds but thick black smoke from innumerable chimneys.

From Rochdale John took the steam tram to Bury and from there he travelled on the East Lancashire Railway through the Rossendale Valley towards Blackington. The valley was a mixture of wild moorland, coalmines, and cotton mills, producing millions of tons of yarn each year.

As the train approached Blackington the landscape became less hilly. Thirty years ago, there had been two villages here with less than five thousand inhabitants but now there was a thriving town of more than forty thousand people, spinning, weaving, dyeing and printing cotton. The centre of the town was rather grand with fine stone buildings and pleasant recreation grounds. But the stone was spoiled with soot and always in the background there was the dull thunder of machinery and a shroud of smoke.

John was discovering that his salary barely covered his living expenses and this visit to Lancashire was going to eat into his funds, so it was important that he find a cheap place to stay. He left the civic grandeur of the town centre and made for the suburbs where the terraced streets were narrower and the houses were smaller and almost indistinguishable one from another.

It had taken most of the day for John to get here. Now it was dusk and the lamps were being lit. Suddenly, a siren sounded, the gates of the nearest mill opened and very soon the street was full of people, drably dressed, often dirty, flowing along the street like a human tide. John was forced to step back into a doorway to let them pass. Some of the passers-by were as young as his pupils back at Hope. John was shocked to notice that a few of these millworkers were missing fingers or hands and one a whole arm. All were pale, thin and drawn.

Suddenly, the wide door John was standing in front of opened and a small fierce man faced him.

'Am thee cooming in or gooing out, lad? For at present you'm just blocking bloody doorway.'

'What is this place?' asked John.

'Temperance Hotel. Were you looking for somewhere to stay?'

'Well, yes, I was.'

'Coom in then. We're not grand but we're clean.'

John took a small room overlooking the street. It was not as cheap as he had hoped, but the landlord explained that he was lucky to get a room at all. There were very few places to stay in Blackington because the population had grown much faster than the buildings to house them. John was provided with a simple meal, rather like a thick broth, with a small amount of meat but mostly vegetables under a topping of sliced potato, browned in the oven, and very tasty.

When he'd finished, John asked the landlord if he knew where Trafalgar Place might be. The landlord frowned. Trafalgar Place was down by the canal in one of the least desirable parts of town, but he agreed to show John the way in the morning. With that promise John made his way to his room and slept soundly.

TWENTY-EIGHT

Trafalgar Place was a poor memorial for that famous victory. It was a small square with terraced houses on three sides and the canal on the fourth. These houses were dwarfed by an enormous mill with black smoke billowing from its tall chimneys. A gutter ran down the centre of the cobbled square, full of dirty water and rubbish. The morning mist had not yet cleared and the smells of soot and dampness clung in it. John was reminded of the East End, where he had trained to be a missionary, except that here, in Blackington, the people emerging from the little houses had an air of purpose about them. There were no dispirited groups of people with nowhere to go and nothing to do; in fact, the whole town appeared lively and bustling. Conditions might be harsh and wages low, but there was work to be had in those roaring mills for all who sought it.

Number twenty-nine stood out from the other houses in the terrace; it had the cleanest doorstep and the brightest curtains, even the window panes seemed to shine. John paused for a moment, remembering that if the people inside were connected to Miss Owen, then he had the worst kind of news for them. At last, he summoned up the courage to knock on the door and the woman who opened it was as clean and neat as the house she lived in, and so tiny that her head barely reached John's chest. Her greying hair was pinned neatly into a bun and when she lifted her face it shone as if it had been scrubbed with the same vigour as the doorstep; but it was her eyes, so similar to those in that photograph of Harriet and her pupils, which told him at once who she was.

'Well, young man, are you going to stand there staring at me all day, or tell me who you are and what you want?'

John was so astonished by her directness that he was temporarily silenced. There was a lilt to her voice that did not sound as if she came from this locality. The woman crossed her arms over her clean white apron and demanded, 'Well?'

He tried to think how he might introduce himself without blurting out his bad news.

'I... I have travelled from Hope Underhill. I have news for you.'

'News? About my lass?'

He nodded.

'Then you'd better come in.'

She led him into a tiny room, as warm and welcoming as it could be made. At a table in the centre of the room sat a small boy, reading a book. The boy looked up at him and smiled. John did not doubt for a moment that he had found the person to whom the locket must be given. This was the face in the photograph, perhaps a year or so older, but obviously the same.

'This must be G—'

'Aye, that's George. And you are?'

'John Noble. I took over Miss Owen's position at the school. She left some of her things at the schoolhouse. I have come to return them.'

'Oh. And what's this news you have?'

John looked anxiously across at the little boy. He seemed totally absorbed in his book, but the woman caught his meaning and her face turned pale. She went to the boy and tousled his dark curls.

'Georgie lad. Would you do me a favour?'

'Aye, Granny. Course I will. Just let me finish this page first.'

She waited a moment till the lad finished the page, then explained, 'You see, Georgie, this gentleman has come a long way to see me and I want to mash him a pot o' tea, but there's none left in the caddy. Take this,' she took a couple of coins from her apron pocket, 'and pop down to Burstons. Ask for two ounces o' tea. All right?'

The boy nodded and smiled and hurried out. The woman asked John to sit down, then went to a chest of drawers and took out a letter. She sat opposite him, unfolded the letter and passed it across to him.

'That's the last I heard from Harriet.'

"The School House,

Hope Underhill, 12th August 1879

Dearest Mam,

I have decided to leave the village and have given notice at the school. I cannot explain yet, but everything is fine and I shall contact you again very soon. Meanwhile, please do not write to anyone in the village."

The first thing that struck John, was that this had been written in the same hand as that letter to the rector, and it was not Harriet Owen's.

'You are Harriet's mother?'

'Yes.'

'And the boy?'

'He's her son. How did you know his name?'

'I only knew that it began with G. You see I found your daughter's locket. I have it with me here.'

The woman sat very still. All the energy had gone out of her.

'Mr Noble. I know your news is bad. I think I knew something terrible had happened from the day that letter came. It seemed so strange for her to want to leave Hope so sudden like. And I knew this weren't her handwriting. Whatever you have to tell me, tell me quick, so I can be more myself when the lad gets back.'

She looked straight at John with glistening eyes.

'Your daughter is dead.'

There was a long pause. The woman drew in a long breath, then gave it out again.

'How? How did she die?'

'She was found in a field. Someone had killed her.'

The woman got up suddenly, upsetting her chair, and ran into the little scullery and began to moan. John did not follow her. He knew that she would want to deal with her anguish by herself. The moaning became louder, then there was the splash of water before she returned wiping her face with her apron.

'But who would... Why?'

She was shaking now. She picked up the chair and set it back at the table.

'Who did this terrible deed?'

'Well,' John began, 'the police think they know who did it, but...'

'You have other ideas?'

'Yes.'

He was about to continue, but at that moment there was the sound of boots on the cobbles and the door latch clicked. George entered and held the small parcel of tea up to his grandmother.

'Here y'are, Gran. There was a ha'penny change.'

Incredibly the woman pulled herself together, smiled at the boy and took the change from him.

'Right then, we'll have that tea,' and before John could object, she was off to the scullery. The boy returned to his book, which looked quite old, and well worn, but with large, clear print and beautiful illustrations. John leaned across and saw the names Tom and Becky and remembered his own pleasure when he'd first read Mark Twain's book, but he would have been quite a few years older than this boy before he could have managed it.

'How old are you, George?'

'I shall be five next birthday.'

'And who taught you to read?'

'Me mam. And Grandma.'

The woman came back carrying a tray with the tea things. The teacups rattled as she put it down on the table.

'How long has George been able to read?' asked John.

'A while. He goes to school in the afternoons. Of course, he's way ahead of the others, but it's good for him to mix.' She passed John his cup. 'In fact, he'll be going this afternoon. I was wondering like if you could you come and see me then? I've a deal to ask you yet.'

'Of course,' he agreed. 'What time should I return?'

'Just after two.'

'Very well.' John sipped his tea, then remembered Harriet's things. He opened his case, took out a small bag and handed it to the woman. 'By the way,' he asked softly, 'I don't yet know your name?'

'My name's Megan. Then Owen, same as me daughter. She went back to her maiden name when... Well, we'll talk later.'

TWENTY-NINE

It was obvious when John returned that Mrs Owen had been releasing her grief while no one was around. She sat him down at the table and studied him with red-rimmed but tearless eyes.

'Now, Mr Noble, I want to know all that happened. No sugarin' the pill. Just straight. All right.'

John told her the whole story as he knew it, from finding the body in the barley field to the inquest and the funeral. He told her about the police suspect and his passage to America. She listened intently, her eyes glistening with tears when he told her about the children at the graveside. When he had finished there was a pause, then she simply said, 'My poor lass. Always the unlucky one.'

Silence hung in the room, dark and heavy as the smoke above the town, until Mrs Owen spoke again. 'So, Mr Noble, why should you be so interested in who did this terrible thing?'

'Because I have taken her place, I suppose. And because I was there when her body was found. And perhaps because she was so much admired. But mostly, perhaps, because I want the truth.'

'She were always much admired,' the woman said, her mouth twisting into an ironic smile. 'Much good did it do her!'

'Did your daughter ever talk about the people she met in the village?'

'Yes. There were that Mrs Bywater. She thought a good deal of her. Then there were reverend somebody. He was quite kind she said, but a bit odd. And she often talked about the children. She seemed to love them all. But Harriet always had a big heart.' Again, that ironic smile.

'One thing that really puzzles me,' said John. 'How did she ever come to be in Hope? I mean, so far away from you? And George?'

''Tis a long story,' said Mrs Owen with a sigh.

'Please,' he said, 'I need to know as much as possible. If I am ever to find the real culprit. And it might do you good to tell me about her.'

'Very well,' she said, 'but I'll need to wet my whistle 'afore I begin.'

Mrs Owen hurried into the scullery, perhaps to make more tea, perhaps to let her tears flow again unseen, perhaps both. John got up quietly from his seat and looked at the photographs on the chest of drawers. There was one picture of a little girl, taken in the days when photography was still primitive, but already the sitter was remarkably pretty, smiling out from a mass of dark curls. Then there was Harriet's wedding photograph, with the bridegroom removed. The last picture showed a proud young mother holding her baby. Looking closely John thought, perhaps, there was a touch of sadness in those large bright eyes.

Mrs Owen brought in the tea tray and sat down opposite John, who began by asking, 'You said your daughter was always unlucky. What did you mean?'

'Well, for a start, she were born at a bad time. You'll have heard perhaps of the cotton famine. They had that falling out o'er slavery in America so the cotton didn't come to Lancashire. We all agreed with Mr Lincoln about slavery, but it meant damned hard times for us. No cotton, no work. No work, no food. Simple as that! It were the young'ns and the oldest suffered most. Harriet got ill when she were three and we all thought she were like to die, but it were her dad died instead. So, there I was, with two lads and a girl to feed and no one but myself to earn a wage. I went back to the mill, which were just pickin' up again. The lads joined me soon as they were able and we got through, just about.'

Mrs Owen, sipped her tea.

'Next few years were better. Me and the lads earning and Harriet growing up fast. The lads loved her that much. She were such a bonny lass and very clever. Even 'afore she went to school we knew that. When she got to eleven or twelve, I thought she ought to go into service, or join me in the mill, but her brothers wouldn't 'ave it. She stayed on at school as pupil-teacher like, and

185

then went to college to be a proper teacher. Ay, it was all going well. Too well.'

Mrs Owen went to the dresser and brought out another photograph. She looked at it for a moment, unable this time to restrain her tears, and passed it to John.

There was Harriet, nineteen or twenty perhaps, standing in the sunlight, looking straight at the camera, smiling at the photographer and the world. It was a good picture, taken by someone who knew how to get the best out of the subject and use light and shade to advantage. She was beautiful. Those thick dark curls falling on to her shoulders and her lovely features firm and clear.

'*He* took that photograph. Her next bit of bad luck!'

John finished his tea and put down the cup.

'She'd finished at college and taken a post in Burnville where she met a chap called William Dyson. Fell for him straight away. And at first it was all right. He were handsome, clever like herself, going places people said. Worked in the mill, but not just a weaver, he was in charge of the machines, keeping 'm going. Important fella. Well paid an' all. Soon he come askin' could he marry her. I'd no reason to object. The lads 'ad gone by now; one to Canada, the other to Australia. Both sent me a bit of money, regular, as they still do, so I were all right.'

The woman paused, then continued quietly, 'It were just after Georgie were born that it all started to go wrong. She'd had to leave her teaching post, and there were only his wage, but it were a good one, so they managed. But William had got himself mixed up with politics. There was a strike at the mill and he was one of the ringleaders. When strike were over he weren't let back. So, there they were, the three on 'em and no money coming in. He tried to get another job but he were on the blacklist. Then he started drinkin'.

'One day Harriet turned up here, out of the blue, wi' Georgie. I suppose 'e must have been about two-year-old b' then. She told me William had started knockin' her about when he were drunk. Showed me the bruises. Said she were leavin' him. I read her riot act. She were his now. A wife belongs to a man. For better 'a worse. She agreed to go back. Said he was always sorry when he was sober again. If only he could get another job things would be all right. I heard no more for a while, but about six months later she were back. This time her eyes were blacked, her arm was broke, but worst of it was he'd beat the lad as well when he tried to stop him hitting his mam. This time I had to let her stay.

'We knew he'd come for her and the lad, so we did a flit, first to Manchester 'cause it's easier to hide in a bigger place, but the only place we could get there were one filthy room, so we came back to Blackington, but another part of town. Then William took his own life and it were in papers about how she'd left her husband and taken his child and that were the cause of his suicide. She was seen as the villain, the one who had

187

deserted her husband, whatever he might 'ave done to her, and that were enough for most folk. She tried to get a teaching post, but soon as they saw the name they said no. So, she went back to her old name, became Mrs Owen. She did no better. Said she were a widow, but they always found out, somehow, who her husband was, and they were always on his side. After all, those managers of schools were always men.

'At last, she decided to try other work, but it was hard for her. She'd not been brought up to do manual work; her hands were too soft, and the other women mocked her "la-di-da' speakin'" as they called it. Then they'd find out who she was and make her life a misery; there was no sympathy for her even though she was a woman. They'd tell the foreman and she'd be given notice. I was doing all I could, takin' washin' and such like, but we were gettin' desperate so she went back to being Miss Owen and wrote to the principal of the college, where she'd trained. By luck he knew about the vacancy at Hope Underhill. She thought p'raps once they saw what a good teacher she was, they'd let her bring George, or p'raps we could pretend he were a poor relation she'd had to adopt. Anyway, off she went and it were hard for her and hard for us, but it might have worked out if...'

Suddenly, the door latch rattled and George came in, red cheeked from running, and smiled at them both. Mrs Owen quickly put on a cheerful face and fetched him a piece of pie she'd baked. She brought John a piece too which he ate and thought it very good. When he had finished his pie, the boy asked, 'May I fetch my book, Gran? It's on my bed.'

'So long as you wash your fingers first. There's a jug of water in the scullery. But don't waste it.'

The boy nodded, washed his hands and went upstairs. When he had gone John asked, 'What you and George need is a little break.'

'What d'you mean?'

'Come back with me to Hope Underhill. See your daughter's grave. Explain things to George. The country air would do him good.'

'How can we?'

'I have a friend who would gladly put you up for a while. She has a young daughter who could keep Georgie company.'

'Well, it's very kind but we can't, it's…'

'Oh, don't worry. I'll pay your fare. And you can pay me back when you can.'

She didn't answer immediately, but when she heard Georgie coming down the stairs she burst out, 'Yes, Mr Noble. I would like that very much. Thank you.'

He could send a telegram to Ella to make the arrangements for their arrival, and if they could get to Manchester by six o'clock there was a South Wales express that would have them in Shrewsbury before ten, just in time to catch the southbound stopping train which would drop them at Churchtown by ten-thirty.

THIRTY

Just as they passed through the ticket barrier there was a deafening hiss and a gush of steam billowed up into the roof space from the brass funnel of the nearest locomotive. George's eyes grew large with wonder at the noise and the bustling crowds in the huge station. He stopped to gaze at the wheels and connecting rods which towered above him, gleaming with hot oil and bubbling water droplets, but John had to hurry him onto the train. As they took their seats and looked through the carriage window, the whole station seemed to move backwards. George had pressed his forehead against the window and smiled as the express gathered speed through the southern suburbs of Manchester, but now he lay fast asleep against his grandmother.

John sat opposite them wondering how it would have been if he and Elizabeth had been blessed with children. What kind of a father would he have made? Would motherhood have given Elizabeth the strength to fight her last illness? Would they have come back to England and settled down somewhere with a growing family around them? It was a long time since he had thought of Elizabeth and his sadness was tinged with guilt.

After Crewe, they had the compartment to themselves. Out of the blue Mrs Owen said, 'I had another visitor come askin' questions about Harriet. Just after Easter it were when this fella came knocking on my door.'

'What was he like?'

''Bout your age. Tall, like you, but much bigger built. Spoke posher than you. Kept his nose in the air, as if I smelt bad.'

John was quite certain who she was describing but wondered how he had managed to find Mrs Owen. Had he seen that slip of paper in the log book too? It seemed very unlikely.

'What did he want?'

'Oh, he wanted to know who I was and did I have a daughter called Harriet. Then he saw George and asked whose child he was.'

'What did you tell him?'

'Nothing! Gave him a flea in his ear. But he just smiled, like he'd worked something out, and left. Never saw him again.'

'Would you recognise him if you did?'

'Oh yes.'

Her eyelids began to droop. It had been quite a day. The rhythm of the wheels on the rails and the gentle swaying of the carriage would soon send her to sleep. John had just one more question. He checked that the boy was truly asleep, then whispered, 'How will you tell George what has happened to his mother?'

'That's not your worry, Mr Noble. You've been very kind. But that's for me to do and no one else. Georgie and I have become very close this last year or so. I'll find a way.'

John turned towards the window, not wanting Mrs Owen to see his tears. She had such courage. He thought of Harriet's body in the field and of the stone stained with her blood. Harriet had indeed been unlucky. He remembered the photograph of her as a young woman and thought of the warmth and beauty she had given to the world. He was more determined than ever to find out who had killed her and bring him, whoever he might be, to justice.

It was well after midnight by the time John returned the dog cart to the hotel and walked back across the hill to the schoolhouse. When they reached Ella's cottage, she had not long received the telegram, but had already put fresh bedclothes on her own bed for George and his grandmother and made up a bed for herself downstairs. She welcomed her visitors as if they were old friends and shooed John away home so that they could all get some sleep.

John was so tired, he just went through the motions the following morning, and his pupils seemed to understand that it would not be worth their while to test his patience. Amy came to school as usual but John did not get a chance to ask about her visitors. He cancelled his lesson with Miss Beale that evening, saying that he was not feeling well, but he could not escape Mrs Bywater's questions as she served his lunch. He gave her the briefest outline of his visit to Lancashire. She was shocked to hear that her beloved Harriet was a widow and that she had a child of almost five but was delighted to hear that John had persuaded Mrs Owen and George to come to Hope Underhill. She wanted to go at once to visit them, but John explained that as part of his plan to find the murderer no one in the village must find out who they really were. Ella would tell people that they were her relatives from Lancashire come to pay a visit.

Mrs Bywater was about to leave the room when she remembered something. She drew two letters from her apron pocket and handed them to John. 'Oh, Mr Noble, I almost forgot. These came while you were away.'

John opened the first letter and read.

"Dear John Noble,

I write to advise you that in my capacity as Diocesan Inspector I shall be visiting Hope Underhill National School on Friday 3rd November to make my annual inspection.

I shall be arriving at 9.30 a.m. and will remain at the school until 12.30p.m. You may then close the school for the remainder of the day.

Yours truly,

Reverend R.M. Dauntless, MA"

Friday! Just two days away. John was glad that this was only the diocesan inspection and not Her Majesty's inspectors, who would decide the financial fate of the school each year. Nevertheless, the inspection could have come at a better time. He had only been in charge of the school for a few weeks and he was least confident about the religious aspect of his teaching. More importantly, he would have to abandon the investigation into Harriet's murder until the inspection was over, and just when he felt ready to confront his chief suspect.

The second letter was from Oakes.

"Mr Noble,

I must inform you that I have received a complaint from Sir Digby Moreton that you are harassing him and his son, Robert. Apparently, you continue to ask questions about the late Miss Harriet Owen. I must remind you that so far as the police are concerned this case is satisfactorily closed and that you would be well advised to cease your enquiries, especially where people of considerable local importance are concerned.

Yours sincerely,
Cyril Oakes,
Acting Sergeant."

Well, well. So, Oakes had received a promotion already. Nothing made John more determined to pursue the matter than being warned off in this way. "People of considerable local importance" indeed! It seemed likely that these would be the same people who had secured Oakes' promotion. Well, damn them all, thought John.

THIRTY-ONE

John had not seen the Reverend Whiting since returning from Lancashire, but he received a note the next day to say that the rector would visit him on Friday evening to discuss the diocesan inspector's report, which the Reverend Dauntless would be leaving with him on Friday afternoon. When he informed Miss Beale of the inspector's impending visit, she was not at all put out. The Reverend Dauntless was one of her father's friends, and anyway, as a committed Christian, religious instruction was one of her strengths.

Another matter was bothering John; he had neglected Ella. It was ten days since the harvest feast and they had hardly spoken since then. It seemed to him that she might think he was using her. He had landed these strangers from Lancashire on her, with only the briefest explanation, and he had been unable to offer Ella any financial help with her boarders, because the trip to Lancashire had left him very short of funds.

When Amy came to school on Friday morning, she placed her school pence on his desk, wrapped in plain paper, and John thought she might have winked at him. When he opened the little package, there was a message written on the inside.

"Please come to the cottage today when the inspector has gone. We have important news.

Your friend, Ella."

John entered the payment into the book, folded the note and put it in his pocket, smiling to himself. At least Ella was still his friend.

The children were subdued that morning. When John had informed them about the inspector's visit, there had been a collective moan. He began the morning prayers and completed the attendance register, while they waited for the inspector. At exactly half past nine, there was a scrape of carriage wheels on the yard outside and a voice like a cannon boomed, 'Twelve-thirty! Sharp!'

When John had seen the name Dauntless at the foot of the inspector's letter it had made him think of a great battleship leaving harbour in full sail, and that was exactly the impression this visitor gave as he strode into the room, his enormous belly preceding him. His booming voice fired the first salvo. 'Good morning to you all.' and the whole school stood. The inspector came to the front and addressed the class.

'You may sit down.'

The children sat in silence.

'My name is Dauntless.'

Someone chuckled. John winced in anticipation of the inspector's wrath. But the man smiled and said,

'Yes, it is a silly name, isn't it? But I had no choice in the matter. My father was saddled with it, so he passed it on to me.' He shook his head in pretended sorrow. 'I expect there are some of you with silly names too. Yes? Oh, don't worry, I won't ask, but I expect we have a boy called Good who is always bad.' Some of the older children saw the joke and chuckled. 'Then there'll be a Bright who isn't.' More children laughed. 'And someone called Groom who wouldn't know one end of a horse from the other.' This time they all laughed; now the man had their complete attention.

What a splendid teacher he would make, thought John.

The inspector shuffled a few paces, adjusted his paunch, and went on.

'Now why am I here? Do you know?'

A hand crept up nervously. Then another and another. The man waited, then chose. He pointed at a tall boy near the back, who looked around, hoping that someone else nearby had been selected. 'Yes, you, the tall boy with the bright eyes. Stand up now and tell me. In case I've forgotten.'

'You 'as come to find out what we knows about God and Jesus an' that.'

'Exactly right. Well done, young man. Now, with your master's permission I shall ask you some questions and ask you to write something for me. I am going to begin the questioning with the little ones, next door. In the meantime, I would like you to write down your favourite story from the Old Testament. Remember now, that's the one that begins with the Creation of the World, then Adam and Eve and that dreadful serpent. Then we have Noah and his ark, Joseph with his fancy coat, Moses in the bulrushes, and the parting of the Red Sea. After that we have David beating Goliath, Jonah and the whale and so many more wonderful stories, eh, and all absolutely true. Well then you choose one and write it in your own words. Just as if you were there at the time. Is that understood?'

There was an enthusiastic reply from the whole class. They seemed eager to begin and wanted to do their very best for this agreeable man. John felt relieved but also suspicious that there might be some catch in it. In his short career he had already met too many HMIs with their poisonous sarcasm and trick questions.

Dauntless whispered to John, 'Do they all have paper and pencils?' John nodded. The inspector turned back to the class. 'Very well! You may begin.' He pulled an enormous half-hunter from his waistcoat pocket and turned to John. 'We'll give them an hour, shall we? While I pop in and see the little ones. I have already met Miss Beale and I have no doubt that I shall find everything satisfactory in there.' He winked at John and passed quickly into the infants' room.

John was left to supervise the class while they wrote their stories. Of course some were soon finished, and sat fidgeting and chewing their pencils, while the more imaginative or more literate developed their stories. While he was quietly pacing about the room John was horrified to notice movement in the long red hair of one of the older girls. He walked on, hoping he had been mistaken, but when he next walked near the girl he saw her scratching behind her ears, and going as close as he dared, he saw several nasty little creatures leaping among the red roots. Well, he would not interrupt her now, or disturb the rest of the class, but he would need to speak to Rachel Downes before she left at the end of the morning.

As he paced the room he could hear low mutterings from next door, where the inspector had softened his tones so as not to frighten his little examinees. When he returned to the big room, he looked well pleased and Miss Beale was beaming. He whispered to John, 'Very good. Very good indeed. Well drilled in their catechism and their knowledge of both the New and Old Testament. You have a very satisfactory assistant, Mr Noble. Now let us see what the older ones have achieved. I am sure we are in for a treat.' Another wink.

'You may put down your pens and read over your stories for a few minutes, then I shall be choosing some of you at random to delight us with your narratives.' In the pause he asked John to pass him the register and when the class seemed ready, he asked, 'Would Andrew Perkins please stand and share his story with us?'

John blanched. Andrew was one of the least able boys; slow and usually tongue tied. Today, however, he showed no hesitation in standing and reading his story, holding his paper up in front of his face.

'There wus this chap called Nohah. God told him it wus gunna rain and rain and rain till the 'ole world wus covered with water. God said he had to build this whackin' big boat and he did and he chucked tar all over it to keep the water out. Then he got two of each of all the hanimals, male and female, you know, like boar and sow, mare an' stallion, and stuck um in this 'ere boat. Then the rain come and Noah and his wife and kids and all them animals floated about on the water for more'n a month. Then it stopped rainin' and Noah sent this raven but it dunt come back, so he sends off this er... pigeon and it cum back with a bit off a tree so they knew there wus land somewhere and then the water started to dry up and they got stuck on this mountain, I think it was called Atarat, so then they unloaded all the animals and filled up the world again.'

Dauntless had closed his eyes during the story. Now he opened them and smiled. 'Well done, Andrew. I think that deserves a clap, don't you?' The whole class applauded and Andrew subsided into his seat with a face redder than the beetroots his mother boiled at home. 'Would you bring me your story out here, Andrew?' asked Dauntless.

'I'd sooner not, sir,' said young Perkins. 'It's all messy like. I ain't a good writer.'

The inspector paused, wondering perhaps whether to press the matter, but then asked another child, a girl this time, to read her story. She read her story of David and Goliath, one of John's favourites, which he had told them only last week, and she had remembered it well.

There was an account of the escape from Egypt, brief but quite exciting, from one of the boys — they all liked the parting of the Red Sea — then a girl read out her rather solemn but generally accurate version of the Creation. After the applause, which the inspector always led, the girl brought her story to the front, then walked back to her desk and sat down again. John was very surprised to see Amy put up her hand. Dauntless saw the raised hand and asked, 'Yes, my dear, what is it?'

Amy stood, her fair cheeks turning scarlet, and said, 'If you please, sir, I don't think that story can be true.'

There was a murmuring among the rest of the class. John gasped. Had his enthusiasm for Darwin caused him to mention that scandalous theory in class or had he talked of it to Ella when Amy was around. He did not remember having done so. Dauntless was shocked but intrigued.

'It sounds as if you have heard of that silly man who thinks we are all descended from monkeys.' He raised his arms and made ape-like noises. The whole class burst out laughing. Amy's blush deepened, but she did not sit down and she continued.

'It's not that, sir. It just seemed like an awful lot to do in only six days.'

John sighed with relief but felt that at some time in the future he might foster Amy's scepticism. His brief glimpse into a future where he might have a father-daughter relationship with the girl surprised but also pleased him.

Dauntless was also pleased. 'Well, there you are. We are talking about a God who can do anything he likes in whatever time he likes. Faith, my dear, is all you need, then it all makes sense. Do you understand?'

Amy stood for a moment, as if she would say more, then nodded uncertainly and sat down. Dauntless took out his watch, studied it and announced, turning to John, 'Ah, I believe that is time for your morning break.' John agreed and the class began to chatter happily. 'Then afterwards I shall be asking some of you to say your catechism.' Worried groans. 'Now off you go.'

John was full of foreboding about the next session. His own lack of enthusiasm had caused him to neglect the more dogmatic side of religious instruction. He desperately hoped that the rector's chaotic lessons had borne some fruit. The children had left the room without clearing their desks and John went to have a look at Andrew's story of the flood. When he lifted the paper there was nothing written on it at all.

THIRTY-TWO

It was almost one o'clock by the time the inspector left and John had had a quick word with red-headed Rachel. He had tried to be diplomatic but the poor girl still rushed away in tears. With an enormous sigh of relief John closed the school, grabbed a hunk of bread and some cheese, and set off towards Ella's cottage. Amy had gone ahead with her friends.

The sky was grey and a north easterly brought brief squalls of chilly rain. As he approached the cottage, the smoke from the chimney was streaming horizontally across the orchard. John turned up the collar of his winter coat and began to regret not stopping to change his shoes, as the path across the field was claggy. It seemed an age ago since that perfect evening when he made his first visit to the cottage.

There was no one about as he climbed over the damp stile, not even Bodger waddling towards him with a warning bark, but as he neared the cottage, he heard the voices of children from inside. He knocked gently and was admitted by Mrs Owen. As he greeted her, he looked about for Ella.

'She's gone up the farm,' said Mrs Owen. 'Mrs Hughes wanted a hand in the dairy. She'll be back soon.'

She returned to a chair near the fire, stepping over Bodger who groaned and stretched closer to the flames, then she took up her sewing and said, 'Making meself useful, as you can see.'

Amy and George sat at the table playing a game of cards. The country air had already put colour in the boy's cheeks. John wondered whether his grandmother had told him yet about his mother, but he could hardly ask her while the boy was around. The game ended with a triumphant 'Snap!' from George, then he leaned close to Amy and whispered something.

'George wants to go out and climb trees.' said Amy.

Mrs Owen lifted her needlework and bit off the cotton, then explained to John, ''Tis his new passion. Since we came 'ere, climbing trees. There's none to climb in Blackington.' Then she turned to Amy. 'Aye, he may, so long as he wraps up warm. And you must take care he doesn't climb too high.'

Amy helped the boy into a warm jacket, wound a scarf around his neck and knotted it snugly. She put on her own coat, patched and faded, but still quite serviceable, while George bounced impatiently around her. Then they were gone.

Once again Mrs Owen read John's thoughts.

'Aye, the lad knows. But he's been so happy here, that it hasn't really got to him yet. And you must remember; he'd hardly seen his mother for a whole year.'

'Have you visited your daughter's grave?'

'We have. Ella took us there this morning. And the strangest thing happened. We were just comin' round the corner of the church when we saw him. This man was standing by her grave. Soon as he saw us coming, he hurried away. But I knew 'im, straight away. It was that fella who came up to Blackington asking questions. Ella said he's the local squire's son, and that we must tell you soon as possible.'

'Do you think he recognised you?'

'I reckon not. He was away that quickly when he heard us coming.'

John paused, thinking. Mrs Owen changed the subject.

'Of course Ella told me that my Harriet were expecting and that the bairn had been dead inside her. So I went to see the little one's grave. Very sad that was.'

After a pause she went on, 'Ella's a lovely lass. And so very kind.'

John felt himself blushing.

'She thinks right highly of you, you know.'

John's blush deepened.

'You'll never know, Mr Noble, how much I appreciate you bringing me here. That were a terrible thing as were done to my daughter. To be found dead in field like that. Done to death by some evil monster. But to see her buried proper, and in such a beautiful place, eases the pain a little. And if you can find out who killed her and bring 'im to justice, it'll give me a little more peace of mind. Will you do that for me, Mr Noble?'

'I'll do my best, and please, call me John.'

Mrs Owen put aside her sewing, stood facing him and reached up to kiss him on the cheek.

'There now, John lad, tha's got two women in thrall.'

Ella returned, looking flushed from the chill air and quite lovely. She gave John a nod and a brief smile but seemed slightly wary of him.

'Have you told him, Gwen?'

'Aye, but he says he'd guessed as much.'

Ella came towards him. He longed to take her in his arms and press his warm lips against her cold cheeks. But she stopped at arm's length, saying, 'Have you thought what you will do now, John?'

'I have to speak to Moreton as soon as possible.'

The colour faded from her face.

'I don't think you should do that.'

John laughed. 'Not you as well!'

Ella looked puzzled. John explained.

'I've had a letter from Oakes warning me not to continue my enquiries, by order of the squire.'

There was a pause, then Mrs Owen spoke. 'Do you mean, Ella, that's there's real danger in this?'

Ella replied almost in a whisper, 'Yes. I believe there might be.'

'Well, then Mr Noble... er John, I agree with Ella. I should much like to know who murdered my daughter, but if it puts you in any sort of danger then let it go. A man who could kill a young defenceless woman like that must be capable of anything.'

THIRTY-THREE

Darkness was falling and John was glad of the lantern Ella had lent him as he made his way back to the village. His visit to the cottage had been reassuring in some ways; Ella and Mrs Owen seemed firm friends and the children were obviously enjoying each other's company, but he was disappointed that he had not had the chance to talk to Ella alone. No more had been said about his investigations and he had made no promises to discontinue them; in fact, he had no intention of doing so.

The wind dropped and the temperature with it. Mist was spreading rapidly across the valley, making it difficult to see ahead, and when John crossed the fields, he took a wrong turning. His head was so filled with thoughts of Ella and his suspicions of Robert Moreton that he had walked a hundred yards or more in the wrong direction before he realised that he was near the barley field where Harriet had met her death. Suddenly, there was a flash, followed by a loud bang, and the glass of the lamp in his hand shattered. He felt the sting of lead shot hitting his legs and heard it flying through the stubble. He dropped the lamp, ran back though the gate and down the lane as fast as he could in the enfolding darkness.

This was a serious turn of events. John sat, trembling, in a chair near the fire, with his trouser legs pulled up to his knees. Luckily most of the shot had done no more than pierce the thick material of his trousers and what had gone through to the flesh was easily dislodged. If the aim had been higher, he might well have lost an eye. Someone out there was prepared to take pot-shots at anyone approaching the squire's land, gamekeepers most likely. He must complete his investigations before someone else got hurt. He changed his trousers and sat thinking about the young woman's murder.

John took out the blood-stained stone from a drawer and cupped it in his palm. He could tell how it would have been held as a weapon, and he imagined a powerful arm bringing it down hard onto a woman's skull. He was convinced that Robert Moreton was involved in the death of Harriet Owen, but he still could not believe that such a man would have committed the deed himself. It was essential to confront him; perhaps even to lay a trap. A plan was just beginning to form in his mind when there was a knock at the door. He placed the stone back on the table, drew down his trouser legs, and went to the door to let in the Reverend Whiting.

It was a calmer, more focused man who entered. He carefully removed his coat and scarf, hanging them on the hook behind the door. John noticed that the rector's suit was clean and pressed and concluded that he must have acquired a new housekeeper. The rector drew a chair out from the table and turned it round, then sitting down he placed a sheaf of papers on his knees and took his spectacles from his jacket pocket. Looking up, he noticed that John appeared rather flushed and raised a handkerchief to his face in case John had a fever.

'Are you not well, John?'

'Oh, no! Nothing like that. I went for a walk. To clear my head after the inspector's visit. I got lost in the mist and found myself in that field where poor Miss Owen was murdered. Someone shot at me!'

'Shot at you?'

'Yes. Luckily, they missed but I heard the shot go by.'

'How close were you to the squire's land?'

'Well, quite close I suppose. The copse borders the field.'

'That explains it then. I have heard that the squire has become much concerned about the increase in poaching. There are people round here who show scant respect for the property of others. The magistrates are kept very busy, I believe. Part of the general laxity of morals I find in this village. It was probably one of the squire's men who thought you were a poacher and fired to frighten you off.'

John's hackles rose.

'Perhaps there are hungry families who feel that the squire can spare a bird or two.'

The Reverend Whiting was shocked.

'We cannot condone theft on any grounds. Remember the commandments. You see, John, I have lately been in great danger of sinning myself. I should never have allowed myself to become infatuated with Harriet Owen. I nearly made a fool of myself. Now it is time to move on. I am determined to forget her. Now, let us attend to the inspector's report.'

In his concern to re-establish his respectability the rector had placed the report on the table behind him. Now he turned to pick it up and saw the stone.

'What is that?'

'Something I found at the scene of the crime. I believe it may have been the murder weapon. It is stained with blood.'

The rector stood, trembling.

'John, you must stop this at once. The woman is dead. Her murderer has been identified.' He pointed to the stone. His voice grew louder. 'Throw that thing away. It's just a dirty old stone. Give up this pointless investigation and get on with your life.'

John lifted the stone in his hand and held it in front of the rector.

'Do you see? There are stains. I believe I am close to finding the man who used it'

The Reverend Whiting became angry.

'John. This has got to stop. You are becoming obsessed. I came here to discuss the important matter of the inspector's report. It is not entirely satisfactory. And if you do not drop this other matter and give proper attention to school business, I may have to inform the managers that you are no longer suitable for the post.'

He went to the door and put on his coat and scarf.

'I must leave you now. I have another appointment. I suggest you study that report carefully and for God's sake get rid of that stone.'

THIRTY-FOUR

When Mrs Bywater came in early next morning, she seemed flustered. She brought John his breakfast, but did not return to the kitchen, standing instead near the table, wringing her hands. John asked, 'What is it Mrs B?'

'Oh, Mr Noble, I 'as a terrible confession to make.'

John laughed. 'Not another shirt ruined, I hope.'

'Oh, no, nothing like that.' She paused, then drew a rather crumpled letter from her apron pocket. ''Tis this. You see, there was three letters come when you were away. I thought I'd given them all to you. Then I come to put summat in me pocket this morning and found this'n. I do 'ope it ain't important.'

When John opened the letter, he recognised his father-in-law's handwriting.

"Dear John,

Thank you for your letter. I was so pleased to hear about your new post and I am sure you will make a great success of it.

As you know I retired at the end of last term. People were very kind and made a collection for me which amounted to a considerable sum, so I have decided to take a holiday. I have just read George Borrow's 'Wild Wales' and have become fascinated by the region, therefore I have booked two rooms at a hotel in Betws-y-Coed (How on earth do you say that?) from the 8th of November. Eunice, our youngest, is to accompany me as Mrs Smithson would not contemplate such a journey at this time of year. Our route to Wales is via Shrewsbury and I cannot think of passing so close without paying you a visit and exploring your famous valley for a few days. I remember how much Elizabeth loved it there. Would you please find us some accommodation nearby from Saturday, 4th until the 8th November. Do not bother to reply, I will assume that you have made the arrangements and Eunice and I will be with you sometime on the 4th. It will be good to see you again. I am sure you will find Eunice much changed since you last saw her.

Yours affectionately,
Thomas"

John looked again at the dates. Today was the fourth! What on earth was he to do? His nonconformist, teetotal guests would not wish to stay at the Swan. And there was no other place in the village with facilities for guests. They might stay in Churchtown, he supposed, but his guests might be here before he had walked there and back. He called to Mrs Bywater, who had crept quietly away into the kitchen while he was reading the letter. She returned, looking as if she might burst into tears when she saw John's face and the letter squeezed tightly in his hand.

'We have a problem, Mrs B. My father-in-law and sister-in-law are arriving today and they are expecting me to have found them some accommodation. What am I to do?'

Mrs Bywater's face changed back at once to her usual jovial expression. 'Why that's not a problem, Mr Noble. I'll make up a bed for your father-in-law in the spare room and the young lady… how old is she?'

John did a quick calculation. 'I suppose she must be… er eighteen or nineteen.' Goodness! Could she really be that old? She was a schoolgirl when he had last seen her.

'Then she can stay with me, in my daughter's room since she's gone into service.' Mrs Bywater smiled smugly and said, 'Well that's sorted out then.'

John stared at Mrs Bywater with astonishment and relief.

'Yes, I suppose it is.'

John had wondered about the wisdom of taking a holiday in Wales at this time of the year, but when he stepped outside, he found that the mist had cleared and the sun was gleaming brightly from a cloudless sky. Perhaps they were in for one of those Indian summers he remembered from his childhood. If so, he would be happy to show Thomas and Eunice the delights of the valley, and to suggest places for them to visit while he was busy with the school. But it did mean that he must again postpone his investigation into the murder of Miss Owen and he would be unable to make a visit to Copse Farm Cottage for several days. With luck he would see Ella at church on Sunday and have a chance to explain.

John thought that he ought to give his parents' grave some attention. The old man who lived in the tiny cottage next to Mrs Bywater had a sign on his gate, "Flours for sale" so John bought some chrysanthemums from him and made his way towards the churchyard. He pulled out the withered remains of his last offering and took them to a damp corner where everyone left their discarded flowers. From here, he had a clear view of the rectory and was surprised to see a carriage waiting at the door and the driver fixing some luggage on the roof.

The rector appeared, dressed for travelling, and got into the carriage, which moved off. Two figures stood on the steps, waving. One was a middle-aged woman, soberly dressed in the mode of a housekeeper and the other was unmistakably a clergyman, but half the Reverend Whiting's age. Perhaps the church had acquired a new curate at last. John wondered what had called the rector away so abruptly or perhaps the arrival of a curate had given him the chance of a much-needed break from his duties. It was strange that he had not mentioned anything of the kind last evening, but he had seemed very distressed by John's attempts to continue the investigation into Harriet's murder.

He returned to his parents' grave and tried to arrange the flowers in the stone vase on top of the grave.

He read his mother's inscription on the gravestone and realised that it should be updated to include his father. He thought, as he usually did at such times, of Elizabeth's grave far away in Africa, wondering whether anyone tended it, or had it been abandoned to the returning jungle.

THIRTY-FIVE

Thomas and Eunice arrived by hackney carriage in mid-afternoon; an expensive way to travel all the way from Shrewsbury, but sensible in the circumstances. Thomas had not changed much, except for his abundant hair, now completely white, like a little snowdrift settled on his weather-beaten head. Those constant rambles through the Fens had kept him trim but his face was quite lined. Eunice, however, was completely changed. She shared none of Elizabeth's heaviness, but taking her father's side, was tall and slim. Intelligence shone from her dark eyes, no longer obscured by spectacles, and her features were handsome. As John helped her down from the carriage, she exuded a confidence quite unexpected in one so young and as she followed John into the schoolhouse Eunice remarked, 'I feel I know this place already; Elizabeth described it so well.' That is astonishing, thought John, for surely, she can only have been a very young girl when Elizabeth came to stay.

John explained about the sleeping arrangements and when they had shared tea, cake and news, he took Eunice and her luggage to Mrs Bywater's cottage while Thomas looked around the school. Afterwards, they took advantage of the pleasant weather to take in the village, beginning with the churchyard, where John pointed out his parents' grave. Eunice took the flowers from the vase, rearranged them more expertly, and replaced them. John hurried them past the grave where Miss Owen's body lay, to show them the ancient yew tree, reputedly more than a thousand years old which would certainly interest Thomas. He did not mention the murder.

John was much surprised when Eunice asked if she might look inside the church. Thomas explained, in a disappointed tone, that Eunice had decided that nonconformity was not for her and that latterly she had begun to worship in the parish church. Eunice grasped her father's hand and smiled. 'I am a great disappointment to my poor father. He is horrified that I prefer the ritual of the established church. As a matter of fact, John, I was hoping that you might accompany me to communion in the morning.'

John agreed to take his sister-in-law to church but told Thomas that he would point out the chapel, so that he might find his own way there in the morning. Thomas strolled round the rest of the churchyard while John and Eunice went inside. She walked at once down the aisle, bowed to the altar and knelt in the front pew for a brief prayer. Returning to John she explained how her conversion to Anglicanism had come about.

'I was in Cambridge for the day and happened to walk into the chapel at King's just as a service was beginning. I was transfixed by the beauty of the building, the candles on the altar, the wonderful music and those age-old words. Our chapel seemed so plain and humdrum after that. So, I began to attend our parish church. It is not as grand as King's, but the building is centuries old and the vicar is quite high.'

John showed her the fine west window of the parish church and the splendid tomb of Sir Edmund and Lady Knightly, local dignitaries from long ago. 'Do you see how they hold hands?' asked John. 'They must have been a devoted couple'

John was shocked when Eunice looked him in the eye and asked, 'What about you, John? My dear sister has been dead for many years and you are still young.

John immediately thought of Ella and blushed but said, 'I have not had time to think of such things.'

Eunice laughed, saying, 'Oh John, you mustn't mind my forwardness. It's just my way.'

Then she took his arm and pulled him back to the church door. 'Come. We had better go back to Father, before I upset you further.'

In the evening, as they enjoyed the simple, filling meal that Mrs Bywater had prepared, John asked Eunice about her future plans. He almost choked on his stew when she said, 'I am going to be an artist. You will have heard perhaps of the Pre-Raphaelite Brotherhood. I much admire their work. I have begun to make tapestries in that style and have been invited to train with William Morris's daughter, May, in London.'

John had never heard of the Pre-Raphaelites but seemed to recognise the name William Morris. He asked, 'What does your father think of that?'

'Her father has no choice in the matter,' said Thomas. 'Eunice has always been a wilful, independent girl. Her mother despairs of her but I say, let her have her head and she will come to see sense at last.'

John was not so sure of this. 'Will she be safe in London?'

'Yes, I shall be safe and well chaperoned by Miss Morris and the other girls.'

John began to feel very provincial and out of touch as Eunice outlined her future.

'Have you always been interested in drawing, Eunice?'

'Oh yes, always. And I have my sketchbook with me. So, if the weather is kind, I shall make some drawings during our stay.'

Next morning, the weather remained fine and sunny. When Thomas left for his walk to chapel, Eunice grabbed John's arm in proprietary fashion and led him off to church. He hoped that they might meet Ella so that he could introduce her to his sister-in-law, but she was nowhere to be seen.

As they walked along in the November sunlight, John explained about the rector going away, and that he was not sure who would be taking the service that morning.

The recently installed organ boomed, its lowest pipes echoing round the old stones. When the choir processed towards the stalls, they were followed by the young man John had seen at the rectory. He was not quite as young as John had first thought and he was a fully-fledged clergyman, not just a curate.

He turned to face them and began the service in a lively manner that seemed to lift the congregation, and when the first hymn was announced Eunice sang out in a fine contralto, causing John to turn to her in surprise. She smiled back at him and touched his arm as if to say, 'This is good.' It seemed that her enthusiasm was catching as John had never heard such singing in this church before. It was if the congregation had doubled and when John looked round there did seem to be more people in the church than usual. Surely, word could not have spread so rapidly that Whiting was away. He looked around again and saw Ella, who had arrived late, sitting in a pew near the back. He smiled across at her but she simply lifted her hymn book to her face and went on singing.

The service continued with a lively sermon on forgiveness that kept most of the congregation awake, and as they sang the last hymn John hoped he could get Eunice outside quickly to meet Ella. After the blessing, the organ blared out a lively voluntary, the organist seeming to have caught the mood of the congregation, and John turned to leave, but Eunice still knelt in prayer. At last, she rose, and he followed her into the aisle. He glanced at the pew where Ella had been, but she had already left. He hurried outside, but there was no sign of her. Why had she left so quickly? And where was Amy who usually came to church with her mother?

John went to look for Ella in the churchyard but could not find her. Eunice was still at the church door in earnest conversation with the stand-in preacher. As John approached, he heard Eunice commenting on the text of the sermon and giving her interpretation. He thought he had better get her away from the poor young man as soon as possible, and just at that moment, Thomas arrived. Together, they managed to distract Eunice and remind her that they were due to take an early lunch before visiting Long Hill.

The afternoon walk was a great success. Thomas was astonished at the variety of flora on the hilltop and pressed some of the less familiar specimens into his notebook. Then they sat together on a large stone, watching the buzzards wheeling overhead, while Eunice sketched a group of ponies grazing nearby.

John kept wondering about Ella. Why had she left the church so promptly? Was she trying to avoid him? He would have liked to return to the village via Copse Farm Cottage, but he felt embarrassed about introducing Elizabeth's father to another woman.

That evening, when Eunice had left for Mrs B's cottage and Thomas had gone up to bed, John wrote a brief note for Ella that he would give to Amy at school the following day. But Amy did not come to school the next day, or the next. John was anxious to visit the cottage and discover what had happened but he did not want to appear rude to his visitors.

Thomas had decided that next morning he would like to see the farm where John had lived when Elizabeth had first come to stay, so John told him how to get there and explained that it was now unoccupied. Eunice was going to do some sketching in the church, which Sam Bywater would open especially for her. When Thomas returned from his visit to the farm, he spent the rest of the day helping John with his class. It reminded them both of when John had visited Thomas's school and how that visit had changed John's life.

That evening John gave his guests directions for Devil's Peak where they were to walk next morning, well provisioned by Mrs Bywater. They returned just as John was closing the school. Thomas was tired after the long walk but talked enthusiastically about the strange rock formations and the views of the mountains further west. Eunice was more subdued and at first, John put this down to fatigue, but later that evening, when Thomas had taken his weary limbs to bed, she explained.

'Sometimes I have a feeling about a place. My artistic nature perhaps. Mother laughs at me. Father says it's my psychic side and I must drive it out with a firm belief in God. But I cannot change the way I am. Today, up there, just before we started to walk back, a mist gathered. The place became dark and threatening and I was filled with a sense of foreboding for you, John. You were up there somewhere and you were in danger.'

John felt a chill pass down his spine. He took his sister-in-law's hands in his own. 'You're not the first to feel a sense of evil in that place. It's not called Devil's Peak without reason. But you have no need to worry about me. I am in no danger.'

He tried to dispel the sombre mood by telling Eunice how much he had enjoyed their visit and explaining the arrangements he had made for their departure next day. 'The carter will pick you up at ten o'clock and take you to the station at Churchtown. The train leaves at eleven fifteen and you will be in Shrewsbury by noon. I hope the weather continues favourably for the rest of your holiday.'

But when John accompanied his sister-in-law to Mrs B's cottage the weather had already changed. The stars were dimmed by a freezing fog that was thickening fast. The night was very dark and John was thankful they had only a short distance to walk. He knew these valley fogs of old. Often, at this time of the year they would sweep in overnight from the west and hang about for days. Eunice shuddered and pulled her cloak tight round her shoulders. When they reached the cottage, she did not linger but gave John a quick peck on the cheek and hurried inside.

It had only taken John a few minutes to walk to the cottage and back but when he entered the schoolhouse, he found a folded slip of paper pushed under the door. On the paper was a printed note, written in a crude anonymous script.

IF YOU WANT TO KNOW WHO KILLED HER GO TO THE PLACE WHERE HER BODY WAS FOUND TOMORROW NIGHT AT EIGHT. COME ALONE OR YOU WILL LEARN NOTHING.

THIRTY-SIX

The following morning John asked Miss Beale to oversee his class for a few minutes, so that he could bid farewell to his guests. He wondered whether their journey into Wales was worth the effort, for unless the weather changed, they would see nothing of the grandeur of Snowdonia or anything else. He had enjoyed their visit; he had always felt a great affection for Thomas, and Eunice had grown into an intriguing girl. He would miss them both.

Amy had still not returned to school. He must visit the cottage as soon as possible to find out what had happened. But what about that note? It might be someone's idea of a joke, but if he did not do as it said he would never know. He wanted to solve the mystery but surely such action would be unwise. He had been warned by several people not to pursue the matter. And look what had happened the last time he went into the barley field. Perhaps he should take the note to Churchtown and consult Oakes. He might agree to accompany him to the field, or at least conceal himself nearby. Yes, that would be the wisest thing.

John returned to the school to find his class in chaos. He should not have left a young girl like Miss

Beale, not much older than some of the pupils, to take charge, even for a short time. Miss Beale sat at the teacher's desk in tears. John stormed into the room, bellowed at the children, removed the cane from its hook and lashed out at some of the worst offenders. Agnes returned to the infants. John sank into his chair and gave instructions to the silenced class. He hated to lose his temper and use the cane in that way. It left him with a sense of failure. He had not felt so depressed since his return to Hope Underhill.

The school day seemed to last forever. He apologised to Miss Beale at lunchtime. She accepted his apology but chided him for never being available for the lessons that would help her to become a certificated teacher. The children remained quiet and got on with their work, but there was a surliness among the older boys, especially those with red wheals on their hands. That could lead to rebellion later and would certainly bring a few parents in to see him. He congratulated Agnes on the diocesan inspector's report, which cheered her, and apologised for cancelling her lessons. He admitted that he had much on his mind but he agreed to restart her lessons in earnest tomorrow evening. By then, he would either know who Harriet's killer was or he would have torn up the note and forgotten the whole thing.

At the end of the day John chose the Lord's Prayer and stressed the words that asked forgiveness for those who trespass against us. Though his belief in God had weakened he still felt that the familiar words he had been brought up with had some relevance and power. He let the children go home a little earlier than usual because the fog was thickening again, and strangely they did seem calmer as they made their way home.

When the children had left, John sat for while at his desk with the log book in front of him and wondered how to record the events of the day. He knew that he was supposed to mention any serious misbehaviour and any punishment meted out. But he did not wish any of this to reflect on Miss Beale and he found it difficult to remember who he had actually caned. He flicked back over the entries he had made since he had become master of the school, just over seven weeks ago, and wondered what he had actually achieved.

Most children had made some progress with their reading and writing and he had been able to keep most of them interested most of the time. The average attendance had improved a little, but it was still considerably lower than in Miss Owen's day. There had been no serious indiscipline until today, and he had been indirectly responsible for that.

The diocesan inspection had been satisfactory, but Miss Beale had come out of it best. He wondered if he really was cut out to be a village schoolmaster. He had not made many friends since arriving in the village, except Ella, and something seemed to have gone wrong with that. Often, he felt himself, as a schoolmaster, to be in a social limbo. His education put him on a level with the rector, but he could not imagine being friends with him. The parents of his pupils generally wanted to maintain a certain distance and he knew that he would feel awkward if he tried to mix with the other young men in the public house. He no longer had much in common with his father's old circle, except for Hughes, but he was hardly likely to see much of him, now that he had no children at the school. Eunice's talk of London and the arts had reminded him that there was a whole world out there. Perhaps he had made a mistake in coming back to Hope Underhill.

He put the log book back in the desk without an entry, closed the school and stepped back into the schoolhouse. He looked at the note again. Who could have written it? It must have been someone aware of his comings and goings because the note had been surreptitiously slipped under his door while he was briefly absent. Why must he go to such a lonely place to be told who the murderer was? How did the writer know who the murderer was and why should he be the one to be told? Why had they not contacted the police? There was no logic in it and considerable danger.

John knew that this would probably be a long evening; even if he simply walked to Churchtown and back it would be sensible to do so with a full stomach. He went into the kitchen and served himself a portion of warm broth from a simmering pot that Mrs B. had left on the stove and ate it with home-baked bread and a bottle of ale, which warmed him within and lifted his spirits. He made his decision. He would visit Oakes; they would laugh at the note and destroy it, then he would go on to Copse Hill Cottage and sort things out with Ella.

John dressed warmly and went on his way. The fog had thinned a little and he knew the road so he was able to maintain a reasonable pace. He rather hoped that some other traveller might come along with a gig or cart and offer him a lift but no one seemed to be abroad that evening. Quite often, Long Hill seemed to act as a border line between weather systems. You might have snow on one side and rain on the other or frost in Hope while it was quite balmy in Churchtown, and so, it proved that night. As John descended into Churchtown the fog dispersed and stars began to appear. He made his way straight to the police office and knocked, but it was not Oakes who came to the door. A wiry little man peered up at John. He wore the uniform of a constable but it was several sizes too big.

'I was hoping to speak to Sergeant Oakes.'

'Was you? Well he bain't 'ere.'

'Do you know where I might find him? It is important.'

'Police matter, is it?'

'Well, yes…'

The constable drew himself up to his full height.

'I'm the new constable. Tricket's the name. How can I help?'

'I would prefer to speak to Oakes. He knows the case.'

This did not please Tricket at all. He stretched up a further half inch and tried to look John in the eye.

'Would you? And who might you be?'

'My name is Noble. I'm the master at Hope Underhill School'

'Well, I'll be jiggered. 'Tis you he's gone to see. He got your message.'

'What message?'

'That note you sent. Saying to meet him at Hillbrow Farmhouse at eight o'clock 'cause you 'ad some important information for 'im.'

'Can I see the note?'

''Tis right 'ere. See?'

John saw, at once, that the print was exactly the same as that on his note, and the same pen had been used.

THIRTY-SEVEN

As John climbed the steep hill out of Churchtown, he tried to make sense of things. He had received an anonymous note telling him to go to a certain field at a certain time on a certain night. Oakes had received a note, purporting to be from John, telling him to be at Hillbrow Farm at the same time. John took out his pocket watch and saw by the light of the stars that it was already a quarter past seven. If he really hurried, he might catch up with Oakes, but he would be hard pushed to reach the farmhouse, show Oakes his note and then get both of them to the field by eight. When he reached the top of the hill, he knew he would never get there in time. The fog was so thick that he must slow his pace and peer down at the road to make sure he didn't veer off it. If he left the road anything might happen. He could wander off in completely the wrong direction or find himself going round in circles. He could stumble into one of those deep valleys that cut into the side of Long Hill or fall into one of its notorious bogs, which had claimed many a lost sheep and occasionally a lost traveller.

John walked on laboriously, his head bent low. If only he had brought a lantern, he thought, but he had not taken one to the field as it might make him a target for those trigger-happy gamekeepers on the squire's estate. At last, he sensed that the road had begun to descend. The fog was no less dense and the damp air was beginning to chill him through his thick clothing. He had no idea what the time might be as he could not see his watch. Suddenly, he saw something ahead of him; a tiny flickering light. It could not be too far ahead, otherwise the fog would have obscured it. It must be Oakes. He called out. But there was no answer. The light moved ahead; sometimes it was strong, then it flickered out for a few seconds, before appearing ahead once more. He called again but Oakes did not hear him. Perhaps it was a trick of the fog, not allowing his voice to travel through it. Or perhaps it was not Oakes. At least he had a light to follow now. It must surely lead him safely to the village.

The light moved steadily on downhill. John increased his pace but the light seemed to be moving faster too. The road dropped more steeply, then levelled off, then dropped again. John began to feel that this was not the right road at all. The road from Hope Underhill climbed the side of the valley in a series of hairpin bends, so that carts and wagons could carry their heavy loads to the top, like sailing boats tacking in the wind. This did not seem quite like that road, but the light was leading him on. Surely the traveller ahead of him must be making for some place of habitation. Wherever it was, at least when they got there, John could check his bearings and find his way back to Hillbrow Farm. Suddenly, John realised that he was no longer on a road because his boots were crunching across stubble. Then the light stopped. It seemed to come towards him, then it went out. Something hard and heavy caught him on the side of his head, and he fell to the ground.

Luckily for John he was wearing a thick winter hat to protect him from the cold November winds, and it had given some protection against the blow to his head. He lay still for a moment with his eyes half closed so that his attacker might think him dead. He saw a dark shape standing over him, presumably a man, wearing a long coat, right down to his ankles, and with his face hidden by a scarf. The attacker bent down to inspect his victim and John smelt something on the man's clothes that reminded him… But the man was not convinced that John was dead and decided to make sure. Raising his weapon, a club or truncheon, he prepared to bring it down again on John's skull. John rolled sideways, and the blow caught him on his cheek, a severe stinging blow that made him gasp but brought him to full consciousness. Before the weapon came down again, he managed to scramble away on all fours. The copse was close so he pushed his way through the hedge, thorns ripping at his hands and face, and scrambled into the darkness of the wood. He was hitting his sore head on low branches, cracking his shins on piles of cut timber, and when he could go no further, he collapsed onto a soft carpet of pine needles.

As his breathing relaxed, John listened intently for any sounds that might indicate his attacker's presence, but there was nothing. He lay still, but as his sense of immediate danger lessened the pain in his cheek and in several other parts of his body intensified. He felt his cheek and knew that it was bleeding, though not profusely. He felt weak and nauseous, but at least he was alive and safe.

THIRTY-EIGHT

A light, much brighter than before, then another, and voices.

'He went in 'ere, you say? He canna 'ave got far. This part of the copse ain't been thinned yet.'

'Right. Make a line. Like we was beaters.'

Another voice added, 'Bloody poachers. Shame they don't still 'ang 'em!'

The six men lined up, arm's length apart, a lantern at each end, and began to walk through the copse, beating the undergrowth with stout sticks as they went, but John had already rolled away and was moving quietly through the wood. The noise the gamekeepers were making was useful, because as long as he kept moving away from it he would be safe. It also covered up any noise he might make as he crawled through the copse. It was still a considerable relief when he made it through the trees, and he could see the lights of the manor through the fog.

Now he must decide. Should he follow the edge of the copse until he reached the open moorland, then try to find his way back to village through the fog, or should he seek a hiding place among the outbuildings until he had regained his strength. He tried to stand upright but he ached in every limb, the pain in his head was like a blacksmith's hammer hitting the anvil and his heart felt like it was going to beat its way out of his chest.

John stumbled towards the nearest building, which was silhouetted against the light from the house. He felt his way around the walls until he came to some steps and climbed up them on all fours. There was a door at the top and he thanked the God he did not believe in when he found that it was unlocked. As soon as he opened the door, he smelt hay. He edged his way forward, collapsed into the soft dry grasses, and fell asleep.

John had no idea how long he had been asleep when he heard the creak of a heavy door and saw a light below him. He pushed his body back into the hay and studied his surroundings in the light of a powerful lantern which now swung from one of the beams underneath him. Through the gaps in the floor below he could see the horse drawn vehicles belonging to the manor, a brougham, a gig, even an old-fashioned coach, all lined up and ready for use. And there beside them, was the squire's son, Robert Moreton. John tried to keep completely still but dust from the hay made him want to sneeze and something hard was pressing uncomfortably into his shin. Just as the sneeze became impossible to control Moreton pushed open the barn door and went out again. John released the sneeze and moved his leg away from the sharp-edged object hidden in the hay.

Moments later, Robert Moreton returned, leading a horse. He spoke gently as he urged it into the shafts of a light carriage and fastened the harness. He placed a small travelling bag in the carriage, jumped in, and drove away, leaving the lamp burning below.

The short rest had restored some of John's strength and he knew that he must act quickly. As he got up from the hay, he saw that it was a large trunk that had been pressing painfully against his shin, and in the dim light he could just make out the initials H.O. on the dusty lid. He pushed the clips, the catches were released and he was able to lift the lid. Inside were dresses, petticoats and other items of women's clothing and on top lay a couple of books. One of the books was a collection of poems by Robert Browning and on the flyleaf was written, 'To my dearest Harriet, with fondest love'.

So, it was just as he had suspected. Robert Moreton was the murderer and now he was trying to kill John. When John had managed to escape, Moreton had told his men that a poacher was loose in the copse and set them to catch him.

John consulted his watch. A quarter to eleven! As he made his way down the ladder from the loft he tried to think of a plan. He reckoned that Moreton would probably make for the railway, but there would be no trains for several hours. If John could get a message to Oakes, telling him about the attack that had been made on him, Oakes could telegraph the police in Shrewsbury and keep an eye on Churchtown station. There was just one other possibility. Moreton might cross Devil's Peak and make for one of the little stations on the line to Mid Wales. But a horse and carriage would not make much speed along those narrow roads in this darkness. A horse and rider would make better progress.

John unhooked the lamp from the beam, turned down the wick, carefully made his way outside and stood still for a moment in the cobbled yard. Soon, he heard what he was listening for; the faint whinny of a restless horse. The stables were next door. John quietly opened the door and looked for a suitable mount. As a young man, living on the farm, he had ridden everything from carthorses to donkeys, and in Africa he had usually travelled any long distance by mule. He selected a black stallion which would be virtually invisible in the dark and collected some tack from the stable wall. It reacted with indignation to this stranger saddling him in the middle of the night, but a pat or two on the neck and some kind words soothed him. Soon, horse and rider were trotting down the drive from the manor, and only just in time, as he heard angry shouts and saw lanterns approaching from the copse.

John could see his way quite clearly now and spurred the stallion on to a gallop. Soon he turned back towards Long Hill and up the little lane towards Copse Farm. He dismounted, tied the horse to a gatepost, hurried across the field to the cottage, and banged on the door. Nothing happened. He banged again. At last, a candle flickered within and a woman's voice asked, 'Who is it? What do you want?'

'It's me, John! John Noble. Quickly! Let me in!'

A bolt was withdrawn, a latch clicked and John fell into the room. Ella gazed at his bruised and bleeding face then stepped forward and took him in her arms.

'Oh, John! John!'

He was about to pass out when Ella guided him to a chair and asked, 'John, my dear. What on Earth has happened?'

He opened his mouth to speak but Ella interrupted him. 'No! Wait!' She went to a cupboard and brought out a small brown bottle, removed the cork and held it to his lips. The brandy quickly spread warmth and comfort through his limbs, bringing back some strength. Ella held his head to her breast for a moment, then hearing Mrs Owen coming down the stairs, she pulled away from him and realised that the cloak she had flung over her night clothes was covered in blood.

'Eh, John!' Mrs Owen exclaimed, 'You'm in a right state.'

Ella lifted her nightdress, ripped a strip of fabric from the hem and began to wind it round his forehead.

'We must get you to bed and fetch the doctor.'

John straightened up.

'No, listen. I have discovered the truth. Robert Moreton is the murderer. He tried to kill me tonight. And I have evidence at last, but he is escaping and I must be after him.'

He began to get up. The two women moved forward and tried to restrain him. It was Mrs Owen who spoke.

'No lad, you're goin' nowhere like this.'

But John ignored her.

'Ella, you must go to the farm and wake Hughes. Tell him to go to Hillbrow Farm where Sergeant Oakes may still be waiting. If not, he must go to Churchtown for him. Tell him that I have evidence that Moreton murdered that poor girl. He must stop Moreton boarding a train at Churchtown and warn the police at Shrewsbury. Meanwhile, I have borrowed a horse and shall be going the only other way that Moreton might have gone. Please. You must go! Now!'

The women could see that he would not be stopped. Ella fetched a coat and laced her boots. She thanked God that Mrs Owen was there to watch over the children.

Ella took John's hand as they crossed the garden. By now the fog had shrunk to a thin blanket covering the earth and reaching to their knees like a lake of cloud and stars were glittering brightly in the cold, clear sky. As they walked over the field John asked, 'I wanted to speak to you on Sunday. Why did you hurry away?'

'Because you were with a fine young woman. I thought you had a new friend.'

'Oh, Ella. That was Eunice. My sister-in-law.'

'I wanted to send you a message with Amy. But she did not come to school.'

'I couldn't send her. Her head was crawling with lice.'

John was so relieved that things had not changed between them that he boldly clasped Ella to him. But there was no time for further endearments. John, reluctantly, pulled away from her, untied the horse and leapt into the saddle.

'Now you must go and wake Hughes. I will follow Moreton.'

And with that, he rode away.

THIRTY-NINE

John took the quickest route through the village, along Back Street, and wondered how many of its inhabitants, hearing the sound of hooves at midnight, would think some ghostly rider was abroad. He crossed the bridge and rode past the Swan where even the keenest drinkers had been sent home and all the lights were doused. He looked north briefly along the road to Shrewsbury, then went straight on and began to climb the steep, narrow track towards Devil's Peak. His mount was eager to show its paces and they climbed swiftly, but soon the fog returned and their pace slowed. John had half hoped this might happen as it would slow Moreton too. The track was barely wide enough for even the smallest carriage and the road twisted and turned as it climbed. At the top of the first slope there was a gate, and beyond that lay open moorland leading to the rocky crags of the Devil's Peak.

In the thickening fog, this part of the route was particularly treacherous. There were no hedges and only a few stones set at its edge distinguished the track as it wound across the moorland, curving with the contours of the land. After a few hundred yards, John was forced to dismount and walk from stone to stone. It was a long slog now and he was already weary, having walked so far that night, and the soreness of his head and limbs was beginning to return, but he must hurry on and catch Moreton if he could.

It was obvious to him now that Moreton had sent the note to lure him to his doom. The meeting place had been cleverly chosen, so that another corpse in the field could be explained as a poacher, accidentally killed by the squire's gamekeepers. But John had escaped, Moreton had panicked, and now he was on the run.

John was treading wearily across the dark moor when the horse stopped, lifted its head and neighed. John stood very still and listened. Could it be Moreton's carriage? Had he caught up with him already? His spirits rose and he hurried on as fast as he could through the fog.

Then in the distance, John heard the faintest sound of singing. A cold shiver passed through his body. He had abandoned superstition when he had given up on God, but now, on this blackest night, in this inhospitable place, in his weary state, the distant singing filled him with dread. He stood stock still while the horse pawed the ground, nervously. The singing rose in volume and he saw a light, moving towards him, growing brighter and brighter until. to his relief, he saw a group of working men wearing leather hats, with unlit candles stuck on the brim, marching towards him, singing loudly, and in good harmony, about the blackleg miner.

The men gasped and stopped abruptly when John and his horse loomed out of the fog.

'Bloody 'ell mon. You dinna 'arf give us a start appearin' out of nowhere like that,' the leader exclaimed. 'What d'you want up 'ere in such weather?'

'You're from the mines?' John asked. There were many lead mines on the other side of Devil's Peak, employing hundreds of men who lived in a shanty town to the south. Some had come from as far as Dudley or South Wales to mine the lead.

'Ah, we'm goin' 'ome. Off midnight shift.'

John was direct. 'I'm chasing a murderer. He's trying to escape. Has anyone passed you in a small carriage?'

The men all began to mutter. John asked, 'What is it?'

The leader spoke again. 'There's a carriage in the ditch up the road, bout 'alf a mile, with a wheel off, and a 'orse still in the shafts. We reckoned the driver 'ad gone for 'elp. But there weren't no one on our road, and you 'ent seen 'im, so he must have gone up the path o'er Devil's Peak. Bloody fool, on a night like this.'

John was excited by the news, but also fearful. That path was difficult enough in the day, with boulders and smaller stones tumbling from the crags, and strewn higgledy-piggledy among the bracken and heather, but in the darkness and fog every step would be dangerous.

'That's my man!' John said.

'Reckon you can catch him?' asked another miner.

'There are others on his trail as well. Between us we'll get him.'

'Look, lads,' said their leader. 'Ow 'bout we lend this chap our lantern. He'll be needing it up there. We know's our way 'ome well enough. And who's gunna see better in the dark than a miner?'

The others grunted their assent and John was handed the powerful lantern, for which he thanked them heartily.

'Now, you get goin' and catch the bastard.'

John set off again, much faster now, lantern in one hand, and the reins in the other. He heard the men marching away, singing again, a sadder song this time, their voices fading as the distance grew between them.

John's horse was the first to know that they were near the abandoned carriage. It pricked up its ears, whinnying softly, and was answered from somewhere up ahead where the carriage soon came into view. He hitched his own mount next to Moreton's. At least they will have company, he thought, then he searched for the beginning of the path and set off between the sodden bracken and snagging gorse.

The track was no wider than his own footsteps and only recognisable by the patches of bare earth where other feet had trod before him. It wound around the largest boulders, their quartz seams sparkling in the lamplight, and climbed steadily alongside the rocky outcrops which crested the ridge of the Devil's Peak. He knew he had reached the summit when the path levelled out and the rocky outcrops loomed up beside him as high as fifty feet. His lamp cast disturbing shadows on the sheer faces of these natural outcrops, like huge phantoms.

Suddenly, there was a sound somewhere ahead; a disturbed stone clacked against another. Only a man's boots would move the stones in that way. John called out, 'Moreton, is that you?' but there was no reply. Only the slip of another stone as someone tried to scramble away. John looked up and saw a dull light just ahead. He increased his pace and called out again, 'I'll catch you, Moreton. You can't get away with it.' But when he looked down again, he realised that in those few seconds of inattention he had stepped off the path. He swung his lamp round in a circle but could not find it again. The only thing he could to do was to follow the light, so he looked up to where it bobbed about some way ahead and took a few paces forward. But there was no path, no earth for his feet to step on. Instead, he tumbled into a black abyss, screaming out as he fell, then landed with a thud on the solid earth, winding himself in the process. He felt a searing pain in his left leg and slipped out of consciousness.

FORTY

John felt as though he were rising gently through deep water up to the surface, as he slowly regained consciousness. He opened his eyes and looked around, by the light of his lamp, which had fallen with him, landed on its side and incredibly, remained alight.

He was in a shaft, long abandoned by the look of it, and the walls were covered with lichen and cobwebs. Test shafts had been dug in many places on Devil's Peak, but usually they were filled in if they proved to be unproductive. This shaft was twenty feet or so deep, with an earth floor. John's leg had been bent underneath him as he landed, his thigh bone had cracked and the pain was intense.

'Help! Help!' he shouted.

A voice above him shouted back. 'It's all right. I'm coming down.'

John twisted his head and looked up. He saw another light above him and a figure apparently clinging to the wall of the shaft and slowly climbing down. The man's voice was distorted by the echo in the shaft, but John recognised it at once and called out, 'No! Go away! Keep away from me!'

Moreton shouted down, 'Don't be a fool! I heard you scream. I can help. Who are you?'

John didn't answer. When Moreton reached him, he would finish him off and continue on his way, leaving John's corpse down here where it would probably never be found.

He wondered how Moreton was able to climb down the shaft, then in the flickering light he made out the rungs of an iron ladder close to the wall, half hidden in the lichen, lumpy with rust, and ending about a dozen feet above the ground. Perhaps Moreton would not realise and would drop off the end and catch his head on one of the boulders that had fallen when the filling sank. Or better still, the ladder would come away from the wall and the murderer would fall and break his neck. John looked about him for a weapon and saw a piece of stone small enough to fit in his palm but heavy enough to do some damage. But when he turned on his side and tried to reach it the pain in his leg was so intense that he almost passed out again. He lay back gasping and heard a thump as Moreton landed safely on the earth beside him. The lamp shone on his face.

'Why, it's Mr Noble. The new schoolmaster!'

'You killed her! You tried to kill me. Now I suppose you're going to finish me off.'

In fear for his life, John tried to overcome his pain and reached for the stone. He managed to grasp it and made to fling it, but Moreton held his arm and took away the weapon.

'You're rambling man! Lie still now! Where are you hurt?'

Moreton set his lamp down on the earth floor, reached inside his coat and took out something shiny. Of course, thought John, he has a gun. He will finish me off with that. Well, at least it will be a quick death. But it was not a gun. It was a silver hip flask, which Moreton held to John's lips, saying, 'Drink, man! It will ease the pain.'

As John sipped the brandy, he wondered why Moreton was bothering to ease his pain when he intended to kill him. Next Moreton took off his jacket and eased it under John's head. He brought John's lamp over and set that upright on the floor. Then he seemed to be examining John carefully.

'Ah, I see. Your leg. It's broken. There's no way I can get you out in that state.'

John tried to move himself and the fierce pain shot through him again, causing him to gasp. Moreton offered him the flask again.

'Here, take this. Go on. Take as much as you like.'

'And when I'm thoroughly drunk you can kill me more easily.'

'What? Look! I've never killed anyone in my life. Well, not since my days in the regiment. And then it was kill or be killed.'

Moreton paused, then continued.

'Listen, I have no idea what all this is about, but if you suspect me of doing something terrible, you'd

252

better tell me. We can't move until daylight, so I am going to leave one lamp burning, so that we have some light until day comes. Then I want you to drink enough brandy to dull the pain a little, and you can tell me what it is you think I've done.'

John was confused and disorientated. He took some more brandy and asked, 'Why did you drive off like that tonight?'

'I quarrelled with my father. Again! We have not been getting on for some time. I don't give a damn about the game or the hunting. I mean, here we are almost into the twentieth century and he cares more about all that old-fashioned nonsense than making the estate pay. I have some great plans. I'd like to farm the land in a modern way and build decent homes for the workers. We could make it profitable again and share that profit with the people who do the work.'

Moreton sat with his back against the wall, his eyes glittering in the lamp light.

'I've tried to explain all this to my father many times. I've asked him to let me take over, but he won't have it. He thinks if I have control, I'll sell the land and spend the money. I probably would have done, a few years ago. But I've changed and he can't see it.'

John's pain had eased a little. Perhaps the brandy was helping. He took another sip. Moreton went on.

'Tonight, we had a blazing row and father told me he was going to cut me out of his will. I decided to leave. Go abroad again. There's an early train from Oswestry that would get me to Chester and then on to Holyhead. So, I set off by the quickest route, but I had no idea the fog was so thick, and then I lost a wheel. Caught it on one of those stones at the edge of the road. The sensible thing would have been to go back to Hope and start out again tomorrow, but I was so angry and frustrated I didn't want to go back. I decided to walk down to Pontesbury and go on from there in the morning. Then I heard your scream and the rest you know.'

John began to wonder if he really had got it all wrong. But there was the evidence. Harriet's trunk, the attempt on his life. He had to know.

'I had an anonymous note,' began John, 'telling me that if I went to Copse Field at eight o'clock tonight, I would learn the truth about Harriet Owen's death.'

'But surely that has been explained. The travelling man?'

'I never believed that. And the further I went with my investigations, the more they pointed to you.'

'Me? But I loved her. Harriet was the only woman I ever really loved. I was devastated when she was killed. We were about to go away together.'

Suddenly, it made sense. Moreton's attendance at the inquest and the funeral. His disappearance for a while to grieve for her. The luggage in the hayloft. Moreton went on.

'Look, we need to get you home and get that leg

seen to. Then I'll tell you all about Harriet and me. But please believe me when I say, I truly loved her. I would never have harmed her.'

FORTY-ONE

When John woke again, he was alone. The lamp had gone out, but there was a tiny circle of blue above him and watery sunlight was filtering down into the shaft. He pulled himself up into a sitting position and looked around. He could not see any way to get out of the shaft, even in the daylight. His leg was still incredibly painful. He looked at the rusting ladder and wondered how Moreton had managed to reach the bottom rung to climb out again. It must have been a dream. He sank back onto the earth. Was he destined to die down there?

Voices! Faint voices high above him. One of them called down the shaft, 'Are you all right, John? We've come to get you out.'

Oh, the joy, the relief. He was not to lie here and die after all. But how would they manage to get him to the surface? He looked up and saw two men climbing quickly down the ladder, as if this was something they did every day. One had a large coil of rope around his shoulders, the other had a roll of cloth wrapped round his waist, like a thick belt. Each man dropped neatly off the end of the ladder and looked down at him.

'Right. We'll 'ave you out in no time. But it's going to 'urt, I can promise you that.'

John knew from their clothing, their sinewy bodies and the confident way they moved about the shaft that these men were miners. He nodded a greeting as tears of gratitude filled his eyes.

'We got to get you to stand up, so we can get this 'arness on you. This part goes round your chest and that bit between your legs. Then we joins 'em up, fixes this rope on and up you go.'

They seemed to know exactly what they were doing, and John had complete trust in his rescuers.

'If you looks up you'll see they've fixed a 'uge piece of timber across the shaft. That's so, when they pull you up, you should stay in the middle of the shaft and not swing into the walls. Got it?'

John nodded again. He seemed to have been struck dumb. One man put an arm under each shoulder and lifted him upright. Tears came again, but this time from the pain that made him gasp for breath.

The other man quickly fastened the harness round him, fixed the rope to the harness and called up, 'Right oh! 'eave away!'

John managed to mutter, 'Thank you,' then he felt his body lifting off the ground and spinning slowly as he rose up the shaft. He could hear other men calling out as they heaved on the rope. John began to feel giddy. He closed his eyes until the spinning stopped and several strong arms reached out to lift him onto the ground.

He was carried away by four more miners. He dropped in and out of consciousness as the men stepped around the boulders and occasionally slipped on the slope. At last, they reached the road and he was carefully lowered onto Moreton's carriage, with its wheel fixed back on. His mount from last night was tied behind the carriage and Moreton leapt up to take the reins of the horse between the shafts. John heard him saying, 'Thank you, men. You have been wonderful. My friend is in no state to show his gratitude, but please share this among you.' He heard the chink of coins and muttered thanks, then the carriage jerked forward.

'How will the others get out of the shaft?' John called out.

'Same way as you did, John.' Then he added, 'Do you know, when I got to the mine to ask for help, the foreman told me that the men would have their pay docked for the time they spent helping you, but they all volunteered nevertheless.'

John was stunned.

'Anyway, I gave them more than they would earn in a week.'

'How can I ever pay you back?'

'No need, John. It was in part my fault.'

'How did you manage to get out of the shaft? The bottom of the ladder was above your reach.'

'Ah, well you see, after Harriet's death I went away to the Alps and learned how to climb. I was shown how to use the smallest handholds, by expert climbers. You look for the least crack or crevice. I used the gaps between the bricks where the mortar had crumbled.

Then it's all about balance. Perhaps one day I can show you.'

'Not for a while,' said John softly. The pain in his leg had begun to gnaw at him again.

'Don't worry about the leg, John. Doctor McKenzie's waiting at the schoolhouse to deal with it. I believe he's going to try out some new-fangled stuff that stops you feeling the pain while he fixes it.'

'What about the school?'

'The children have been sent home. School will be closed for a few days. The rector saw to that. He's waiting to see you. In fact, you have quite a reception committee waiting. One of them is a pretty young woman who has been quite distraught all night.'

John smiled to himself as the carriage swayed on down the hill, then pain and fatigue overwhelmed him and he passed out again.

FORTY-TWO

John was carried straight to his bed. Mrs Bywater had laid an old sheet on it for Doctor McKenzie had warned her that the new process of encasing the leg in plaster of Paris would be messy. McKenzie may be stuck out in the backwoods but he tried to keep up with the latest developments in medicine, especially if he could charge a good fee for the service. Robert Moreton had already offered to pay for the treatment and John would just be charged a nominal amount.

John was barely conscious when McKenzie came upstairs followed by Mrs Bywater carrying a large bowl of water. The constant pain of the last few hours and the overall strain of such an eventful night had left him totally exhausted. He heard the doctor's voice and tried to concentrate on what he was being told.

'Well, John, you're a damn fool and I've nay sympathy for your predicament. T'was a foolish adventure you set upon. In the best of circumstances, the fracture of your right femur should have been set at once. It will now require considerable manipulation with a consequent increase in pain. But you're a lucky man, for I have the means to put you to sleep while I set the leg and you will, therefore, feel nothing. A certain physician called Simpson, a Scot naturally, has given us something called anaesthetic. That's A-N-A-E-S-T-H-E-T-I-C. And if I fix this wee pipe into the jar and place this mask over your face you will…'

When he woke again John was certain that he had gone to heaven. Certainly, there was an angel sitting by the window with celestial light playing through her golden hair. He blinked and licked his lips, which were very dry, and hearing him stir, the angel moved towards him.

'John, my dear, you are back with us again. Thank God.'

His head ached and he felt as if he might be sick at any moment. The angel came close and took his hands in hers. They were not insubstantial as he thought an angel's might be, but firm and warm and comforting.

'Where am…'

'In your bed in the schoolhouse. You've slept through a whole day and night, John. Now you must drink.'

The angel offered him a glass of water and he drank greedily. His head cleared a little, the room came into focus and he remembered.

'My leg?'

'It's covered in plaster to keep the bones in place, John. Doctor McKenzie says that because you are a healthy young man the fracture will mend in a few weeks. Then the plaster can be removed and you'll be as good as new.'

'What about the school?'

'It is closed for a few days, except for the infants. Miss Beale is managing them. I have been helping out too.'

'How soon will I…'

'You should be able to get up in a day or so. Then we'll have you downstairs. Doctor McKenzie has brought you some crutches so you'll be able to hobble about.'

'Oh, Ella. There's no one else I would rather have seen when I woke up. You are an angel.'

Ella blushed and laughed.

''Tis Mrs Bywater you really have to thank. She was here beside you most of the time.'

John held out his hand and Ella took it. He pulled her willingly towards him to kiss her, but at that moment there were heavy footsteps on the wooden stair, a powerful tap on the door and Oakes entered.

John gave a slight smile but said nothing. Oakes looked thoroughly official but rather uncomfortable in his new sergeant's uniform.

'Do sit down, Sergeant. There's a chair by the window. By the way, Oakes, I believe that congratulations are in order.'

'I have not come here to discuss my career, Mr Noble, or my personal life. In fact, I am 'ere to pick a very large bone with you, and to consider whether I ought to charge you with wastin' police time.'

'Oh, I see. Well while you're considering the matter, I wonder if you could tell me what actually happened the other night.'

'I suppose you have a right to know in case I have to make it an official matter. Now then, first there was that note.'

'Ah yes, Tricket told me about that.'

'*Constable* Tricket had no right to show it to you but let that be for the present. Anyways, I did as the note said and made my way to Hillbrow Farm.

'It were a terrible night as you know, so I may 'ave been a bit late, but you wunna there anyways. I waited a good while, then I come down to the schoolhouse but you weren't there neither, so I tried the rectory but the housekeeper said the rector'd been away for a few days. Next, I called on Mrs Bywater who told me she anna seen you since the morning, when you'd seen off them visitors of your'n, but she said you'd probably be back soon and would I like to step inside for a while and wait. Naturally, being the generous woman that she is, I were offered a cuppa and a piece of that splendid cake she bakes. But after an hour or so, I reckoned it weren't fair to bother 'er no more, so I left and went down to the Swan. Thought I'd ask about a bit, see if anyone had seen you, but no one had. Well, all that police work give me a thirst so I had a pint or two. And not long after that the landlord called time. Round about eleven that would 'ave been. You 'adna got back to the schoolhouse so I thought, well that's it then, someone's playing silly buggers, so I set off 'ome. Then just as I was passin' the end of Manor Lane, I met Hughes, with his 'orse and cart, tearin' down the road in a terrible 'urry.'

'Oh, I knew he would do it. He's a good man.'

'How *I* see it is this. You had 'alf the village running about in the middle of the night just 'cause you had an idea you'd found a murderer, when in fact, you was just harassing an innocent man. Anyways, Hughes took me to Churchtown in his cart. I sent Tricket down to the station to watch for Moreton. I telegraphs Shoosbry to warn 'em to keep a look out up there. Then me and Hughes come back 'ere. We drives about a bit, but there's no sign of you or Moreton. After that we all gathered at the schoolhouse and waited. By then 'tis almost daylight and soon after we see your murderer coming along in his carriage. I goes to arrest him, but he points to you lying in the back. Hughes and me carries you up 'ere then he goes off to fetch the doctor and I returns to Churchtown. As I say, half the village, up all night just 'cause you gets a mad idea in your head. Now, I wunna say I'm takin' it further and wunt say I'm not, but if you start on about this bloody murder again, I'll 'ave you in clink afore your feet touch the ground, well, that is, when that un's mended. Now listen up, John Noble, and listen good. Young Harriet Owen was murdered by that wandering vagabond. The case is closed.'

'So, who sent those notes? And who tried to kill me?'

'You were most likely attacked by the squire's men because they thought you were a poacher. And as to those notes. I 'as no idea. Perhaps you sent 'em yourself.'

Perhaps it was his weariness or perhaps he too had begun to have doubts, but John had no energy left for further argument.

'Right, now I've got some important matters to deal with. Forget that bloody murder, John Noble. Do I make myself clear?

John nodded.

'Right then, I'll be orf. And you get back in that school quick, before I 'as a load of idle lads and lasses up to no good.'

Oakes carefully set his helmet on his head, then nearly knocked it off again as he went out through the door and clattered downstairs.

John slept again and had a strange dream. He saw Harriet standing among the uncut barley in that field. It was the Harriet of the photograph, young, beautiful, smiling, in her white dress and with her hands held out towards him. He walked towards her, reaching out, but when their fingers should have met, she disappeared and he tumbled forward onto the ground. Darkness descended like folds of thick cloth, almost suffocating him and there was that strange smell again.

He was sweating when he woke. He lay still in the quiet room trying to sort out his thoughts, but soon he heard more footsteps on the stairs. His next visitor was Robert Moreton.

'Look, John, I know I have a reputation. And some of it is true. I like women, pretty women, fascinating women. And they seem to like me. It became a sort of drug, a temporary comfort. But Harriet was different. The moment I met her at some event in the village, I fell completely under her spell. Eventually, I asked her to marry me. She was not of my class, but we could have gone away, abroad even, where such things matter less. But she said she could not marry me. For some reason, it was impossible and I couldn't understand why. One day, I found a telegram she had received, with the address of the issuing office on it. I went up there, to a place called Blackington, and bribed the clerk to show me the sender's receipt. I found the place, asked a few questions and found out about Harriet's husband and her child. I was angry when I got back. I felt that she had deceived me. I said that I would tell the managers and get her removed from her post. She begged me not to, so I agreed, and in return, she agreed to be my friend, and meet me from time to time. We used to meet in secret at your father's old house.

'Gradually, things changed between us. It was natural, I suppose. A man and woman meeting in secret. I do have a slight charm and she was a warm, generous woman who had been deprived of physical love for far too long. She became fond of me, enjoyed our meetings, and gradually we became lovers. I said she was a naturally giving person. We became very close.

'Then she told me she was pregnant. I didn't care. I said I would take her away. We would collect her son from Blackington and begin a new life somewhere else. At last, she agreed but she wouldn't leave until the end of the term and she did not want anyone to know about us until we were far away. So, this is what we planned.

'A few days after the term ended, I waited until it was dark then drove the carriage down to the schoolhouse and collected Harriet's things. The next day, she was supposed to walk up to the farm and wait for me. At midnight, I would drive the carriage up the lost road, as they call it, onto Long Hill, cross to the Churchtown Road, then come down to the farm and collect her.'

'Black Powell's chariot!' exclaimed John. 'It was you that Hepzibah heard!'

Robert Moreton did not seem to hear what John had said. He was lost in his own story.

'When I got to the farm, there was no one there. The door was wide open, but Harriet was nowhere to be seen. I searched the gardens, the buildings, the nearest fields. I thought she must have changed her mind. I took her luggage and hid it in the hayloft until I could find her and talk to her. The next day, I went down to the schoolhouse and Mrs Bywater was in quite a state. Harriet had gone out the day before and had not returned.

'I began to wonder if Harriet had had second thoughts or had simply changed her mind and run away from me, but I felt that she must still be nearby. She did not have much money, certainly not enough for a long train journey. If I could find her and talk to her everything would be all right again. I wrote a letter to the rector giving notice on her behalf, and another to her mother telling her not to worry. Then I began looking for her. A few days later, I heard that her body had been found. I was devastated. I went to the inquest and her funeral, then I had to get away. I was in a terrible state.'

John hardly heard the last of Moreton's words, because he drifted off to asleep again. When he woke again there were two figures standing beside his bed, a woman and a child.

'We've come to say goodbye.'

It was Mrs Owen and George.

'It's not right to impose ourselves further on young Ella. She's been that kind. But now we must get back to Blackington.'

John turned to the boy. It was almost the first time he had seen his face without a smile.

'George?'

'I don't want to go. I like it here. And I shall miss Amy very much. But Grandma wants to go and I must go with her.'

John wondered how such a young boy could be so sensible.

Mrs Owen pulled George to her and gave him a hug. 'It's not so much that I want to go, but there's rent to be paid or we shall lose our home. And George must get back to school. Harriet would have wanted that.'

John nodded.

'I know that my daughter is at peace in a lovely place. And Ella has told me she will look after the grave.'

'What about Harriet's things that I found in the hayloft? Did anyone tell you?'

'Aye. That young man Robert brought them round. I've given Ella the best dresses. She and Harriet were much the same size.'

At that moment, there were more footsteps on the stairs and the Reverend Whiting appeared.

'Good day, John. I'm sorry to disturb you and your visitors but I need to speak to you urgently.'

'It's all right, Rector. We were just leaving. So, you must be Reverend Whiting. My daughter often spoke of you.'

The rector blushed and shook Mrs Owen's hand coldly.

'This is my daughter's little boy. His name is George.'

Another brief, cold handshake. George had been staring at Whiting ever since he came into the room. Now he asked, 'Mister, why are you wearing a frock?'

Whiting looked sharply at the boy.

'This not a frock, boy. I am a priest and these are my priestly vestments. Do you know nothing of the church?'

'Sorry, Rector, we're chapel see,' said Mrs Owen.

'But your daughter. She attended the church.'

'Aye. When in Rome, as she used to say.' And with that, Mrs Owen left with George.

The rector walked across to the window and looked out. The black shape of his cassock silhouetted by the sunlight reminded John of something but he could not quite decide what it was. There was a moment's silence then the rector walked back towards the bed.

'I have a serious matter to discuss with you, John. I have been away for a few days as you know. I went to Oxford to see an old friend.'

'I saw you leave. When did you return?'

'Early yesterday morning. As I was saying, I saw an old friend who knew of you. Apparently, your paths had crossed at some time. He told me of your disastrous African adventure and said that in consequence of your wife's death you had lost your faith. Is that so?'

John brazened it out. 'It's possible.'

'In that case, I do not see how you can remain as master of a church school.'

'But...'

'Besides which your behaviour of late has given me great concern. This ridiculous obsession with Miss Owen's death has distracted you from your work in school. Dauntless was not impressed, not at all

270

impressed with your pupils' knowledge of the catechism. I wanted to discuss the matter with you the other evening, but you were too distracted. I warned you, the squire warned you and Oakes did the same, but you continued to harass people and make ludicrous accusations. So, I have spoken to the managers and they have agreed that you are to be suspended immediately, and that a replacement will be found as soon as possible. You should vacate the schoolhouse within the week. Do I make myself clear?'

John was seething, but he knew that there was no point in arguing. Whiting held all the power.

'I see no reason for us to meet again. You must make your arrangements to leave the schoolhouse and preferably the village.'

With that, Whiting swept out of the room leaving behind a certain smell, which John recognised at last. It had seemed different in the open air, but now he knew for sure what it had been.

FORTY-THREE

Late November. The last leaves had fallen from the oaks
and elms. Winter seemed to have come early. The
temperature rarely rose above freezing, even in the
middle of the day. The first flurries of snow had
whipped across Long Hill, whitening the bracken and
causing the sheep to huddle in groups among the gorse.
Most outdoor farming activities had ceased, except the
dreaded hedging and ditching. The cattle had been
brought in and stood steaming among the mud and straw
in the byre. Driven indoors, the men took the
opportunity to make and mend their equipment for the
following year. There were extra hands to help with
these tasks in Hope Underhill this year because of the
school closure.

With the squire's permission, John was living at
Hillbrow Farm, his old home. Robert had persuaded his
father that John was no danger to him, and it seemed
sensible to have someone living there instead of leaving
the place empty.

Ella had cleaned a couple of rooms downstairs at
the farm and John would sleep there on a truckle bed
until his leg was mended. The managers had agreed to
pay John's salary until the end of the month, but he

would need to find new employment as soon as possible, and that would probably mean moving on again. Meanwhile, he sat in the parlour of his childhood home, thinking about his parents and the good life he had shared with them. Perhaps, if he had stayed with them and taken on the farm things might have been different, better all round perhaps. The more introspective he became the more depressed he felt. Then to cap it all John heard that old Dick had died in the workhouse and had been given a pauper's burial without anyone being informed.

The only time his spirits lifted was when Ella arrived, bringing provisions for him. Usually, Amy accompanied her and while Ella cleaned and tidied, John gave Amy some lessons so that she did not fall too far behind while school was closed. Ella was always cheerful and relaxed when Amy was with her, but alone with John she was more reserved and John began to wonder whether she was tiring of him. He had made so much use of her in one way or another, that perhaps she would be glad when he moved on. Eventually, he decided to talk to her about it.

'I suppose,' Ella began, 'It's the thought of them, Robert and Harriet, being here. Of what they did when they were here.'

'Was it so dreadful? After all they were in love. They were going to go away together. Robert really did mean to marry her.'

'I suppose. But look what it led to. The wages of sin, some would say.'

'I don't believe that Ella. What happened was not their fault. Someone murdered Harriet Owen and I think I know who it was. I dare not mention it, after what happened with Moreton. I need to have absolute proof. But I don't know how to get it yet.'

One evening when Ella came to visit, she was wearing a dress John had not seen her in before. It was similar in style to the blue dress Harriet had been wearing when she died, but this one was pale green. Ella explained that it was one of the dresses from Harriet's chest, given to her by Mrs Owen. At first, she was reluctant to wear it, but Mrs Owen insisted that Harriet would not have wanted it wasted. Ella said the dress fitted her very well though she did not particularly like its colour but it was the kind of material which might easily be dyed when she had more time.

When Ella left that evening, John sat on in the lamplight, thinking yet again about Harriet. What had caused her to run away from this place in such a hurry that August evening? Where had she been making for when she ran out leaving the door ajar? Why had she crossed the barley field and who had been following her?

FORTY-FOUR

It was a miserable Christmas that year for the people of Hope Underhill. The agricultural depression had worsened. A poor harvest and low grain prices meant that the farmers must tighten their belts, and that meant laying off more workers and paying lower wages to those who remained. Ella and Amy had gone to spend Christmas with Mrs Owen in Blackington, so John was usually alone, except when Robert or Hughes came with provisions.

On Christmas Day, he had a visit from Mrs Bywater. He was glad to see her, and the cake she brought, but the trials of the last six months had aged her, and she seemed quite lost without a school to clean and a master or mistress to look after. The worst news was that Miss Beale had moved to another school, where she could have regular lessons in preparation for her examinations, so that even the infants' part of the school was now closed.

John was now convinced that he knew who the murderer was and he was beginning to think of a way to prove it. But proof to him alone was not enough. He must have witnesses. He knew a couple who would support him, but the most important witness would be the most difficult to obtain. Sergeant Oakes must be there, but Oakes was a true sceptic so far as John was concerned; in fact, he had warned off John from continuing his investigation. The only hope was to make a direct personal approach to the man and convince him to be there when the proof was shown.

So, John must make his way to Churchtown on foot and alone. His leg was pretty much healed but would it stand up to a three-mile walk beginning with a strenuous climb? He had made a few practice runs, or rather steady plods into the village; this would be different, but it had to be done, so one afternoon when the wind had dropped and the temperature was somewhat milder he set off.

As he climbed the hill towards Churchtown John thought back over the last six months since he had returned to the village, beginning with that dreadful discovery in the barley field. His tenure as master of the village school had gone reasonably well, but he had been preoccupied with trying to catch the murderer of that poor young woman. He had known at once that Oakes was wrong to suspect that traveller who had stayed with the gipsies for a few nights, but he had come to strongly suspect the young squire, and been proved disastrously wrong, with a broken leg and considerable censure for his pains.

But there had been positives too, especially his growing friendship, in fact more than friendship with Ella, and if he was able to carry out his plan to unmask the murderer, he would need Ella's help. There was also young Amy, who now felt like a daughter to him; his meeting with the remarkable Mrs Owen, who had such strength in adversity, and her bright young grandson, George.

By the time he reached the top of the hill his leg was already causing concern but at least now the road was level. The wind had risen again but it was coming from the west, and his thick coat protected his broad back. A group of ponies watched him pass, then raced off as if he had spooked them. He remembered that tale the old gipsy woman, Hepzibah, had told about the chase across the snow covered hill and the fatal fall of the villain, Black Powell, confused by the light. Just at that moment the clouds parted and watery sunlight streamed through, but the sun was already behind him moving westward and he would need to move faster if he was to make Churchtown before dark.

At last, he saw the little town in the valley below and began the steep descent. His leg was very painful now and he was limping badly. He would just about make it to the police office, but he hoped desperately that Oakes would be in and that he would be able to hire a horse for the return journey.

The last half mile down the valley and into the town was sheer agony but at last he reached the police office and rang the bell. It was that new constable who came to the door. John's heart sank but then he heard a familiar voice calling from inside.

'Who is it, Constable?'

'That schoolmaster chap from Hope Underhill.'

'It's John Noble, Sergeant,' John announced.

'Oh 'im. Bring him in, Constable'.

So John entered the office, limping badly.

'That leg still troubling you, Mr Noble? Your own fault if I might say. But never mind, take a seat. Is this a social call?'

John sat in the offered chair and rubbed his leg. 'No, not social. I have something important to tell you.'

'It must be bloody important if you'm walked all the way here from Hope with a gammy leg. Constable, go and make us some tea.'

When the constable had gone, Oakes smiled and asked, 'So who d'you reckon done it this time?'

'I don't want to tell you but to show you.'

'And you think you've got it right this time?'

'Yes, Sergeant.'

'So what do you want me to do?'

'I want you to be at a certain place at a certain time.'

'Easy as that?'

'Yes, Sergeant.'

'Well, I'll tell you what, John Noble. I'll be there but if you'm wrong this time you'm in deep trouble. It'll be wasting police time, and we takes that very seriously.'

The constable arrived with the tea and set down the mugs on the sergeant's desk.

'Careful with that desk, Constable. It's just been polished.'

They sipped their tea in silence for a while. John was very grateful for the hot sweet drink. He was not sure he would be able to stand again.

'Constable, would you go to the stable and harness up the pony in the cart. When Mr Noble and I have finished our little chat, I'd like you to take him home, then you can get off home yourself.'

John wanted to object, but he just could not face the walk back across Long Hill. The constable left the office.

'I cannot thank you enough, Sergeant.' He passed him a note. 'That tells you when and where. Please don't be late.'

'I must be mad to do this, and I'll warn you again, John. Any nonsense this time and I'll be arresting you for wasting police time.'

John heard the clip-clop of hooves and left the office, saying no more.

FORTY-FIVE

At the beginning of the new year, the weather turned desperately cold. Clear nights made for severe frosts and the brief sunlight of those short days gave little respite. The rector was busy with funerals. The very old and the very poor were particularly vulnerable in winter. But the rector himself was looking better than he had for some time. Apparently, he had been on another visit to Oxford and had seen an old friend, who was reconciled to his unwillingness to be married but in her loneliness was pleased to offer him succour. But he could not remain away from his parish for too long, even though the thought of being back among those stupid parishioners in that cold, bleak, uncivilised place was utterly depressing.

It was his habit to go alone into the church each evening, light a single candle and kneel in prayer. He was sure that these prayers had helped him to cope with all the difficulties of this past year, his loathing of his backward parish, his rejection by Harriet Owen and that heathen, John Noble, who had wormed his way into the village school. Coping with all these problems seemed to have given him new strength and helped him to make up his mind to get away from Hope Underhill and start anew in some comfortable suburb where his parishioners would be of his social class, share his tastes and support a higher style of service. He had already written to the bishop, a recent appointment, and received an encouraging reply.

The rector had not bothered with a lamp this evening because the moon was full and bright enough to show him the familiar path. He unlocked the church door and stepped inside. The chill of the building struck him at once and he was glad he was wearing a thick cloak over his cassock. He felt for the small candle that was always left in a niche beside the door with a box of safety matches. The candle was not there, but the moonlight which had helped him find his way across the churchyard had penetrated the east window and when his eyes adjusted, Whiting was able to make out just enough to find his way to the chancel steps. He felt for a kneeler in the gloom of the front pew, set it on the cold step and closed his eyes.

Praying in stillness and silence, he gradually became aware of a light around him. Whiting was not a superstitious man and his religious life had never reached great spiritual depths, but he began to wonder if perhaps at last some manifestation of the Divine was about to be revealed to him. Slowly the rector opened his eyes and stared in horror. This was no heavenly spirit but an apparition straight from hell.

The candles on the altar were lit and in front of them knelt a woman, with a thick mass of dark brown hair falling over the shoulders of a pale blue dress. He knew her at once and called out, 'You! You deceiver! Fornicator! How dare you come into my church!'

The woman did not turn but spoke in a low voice and a distinctive accent.

'I've a right to be 'ere. After all I'm buried close enough.'

The rector was shaking with dread.

'No! No! This cannot be. This is some terrible joke.'

'It's no joke to be 'it on the head with a heavy stone. To have your skull broken and die among the barley stalks.'

'But you had to die. I could not bear to think of you with him. Doing that! You had to die for your sins. You whore!'

'So, you followed me to the farmhouse and tried to strangle me but you're old and unfit and I escaped. I ran to the manor to find Robert, but my dress got caught on the brambles in the copse, and then I stumbled on a stone in the field. You picked up that stone and…'

'God put that stone in my hand. You had to die so that you could not pollute us all. I had to cleanse the village of you.'

'Well, I've come back. And I'm going to haunt you for the rest of your life. To remind you of what you did.'

'You should be in hell for your sins.'

'If I go to hell we'll be there together because you murdered me. Thou shalt not kill, the commandment says.'

'You deserved to die. I would do the same again.'

'Then why don't you? Look, there on the floor. There's the stone. Pick it up and bring it down on my skull. Perhaps that will send me to hell for ever.'

The rector's whole body trembled. His mind was in turmoil. He could not believe, but there she was, with her luscious brown hair and lilting Lancashire dialect, mocking him.

He picked up the stone, gripped it tightly and moved towards her.

'I wouldn't do that, Reverend, or you might be found guilty of a second murder.'

There were more voices, figures moving towards him, lamps and candles being lit. The rector was surrounded.

He turned to face the apparition, but it began to transform in front of his eyes. The dark curls were being lifted away to reveal a head of blonde hair, and a pair of blue eyes stared at him with contempt. He dropped the stone and collapsed onto the floor; a broken man, moaning loudly.

Oakes pulled the limp figure of Cyril Whiting to his feet and clamped a pair of handcuffs on his wrists. The other men closed in, threateningly, around the rector.

'You bastard!' exclaimed Hughes, raising his fist.

'Now then, Ted! There's a woman present,' Oakes reminded him. Sam Bywater closed in and spat at the rector in front of him.

'I allas thought you were a cold, queer fish, Whiting. May you rot in 'ell.'

'He'll have 'is neck broke in a noose afore that!' said Oakes. 'Up at Shoosbry Gaol!'

The murderer was led away, stumbling over his own feet in his misery.

Meanwhile at the back of the church John struggled to his feet, came towards Ella and took her in his arms.

FORTY-SIX

When they reached the top of Long Hill John steered the trap onto the mossy verge, gently tugged the reins to halt the pony, and leaned across to kiss his bride. All around them on the wild moorland were signs of spring. There were leaves on the wind-bent trees, the slender shoots of new ferns were uncoiling and pushing through the brown blanket of last year's bracken, lambs leapt for the joy of spring and skylarks twisted and shrilled high above them in the clear sky.

It had been a Whitsun wedding and the whole village seemed to have found time to attend the service. Perhaps the villagers were grateful to John for removing the detested rector, who was still housed in Shrewsbury Gaol awaiting execution. Perhaps, they were grateful for his success at the school, where the HMI had recently given him their seal of approval and a slightly increased grant. Or perhaps, they were just happy to see two comparatively young people starting a new life together after the pain and suffering both had endured, especially during the dark days of the previous year.

The new rector, the Reverend Pryce-Jones, with his bright red-hair and explosive laughter, had recovered most of the parishioners lost by his predecessor, so the wedding hymns rang out lustily, disturbing the dust among the ancient rafters of St Mary Magdalene.

Elizabeth's parents put aside any prejudice against the established church, and any feelings they might have about their daughter being replaced by another woman in John's life. They had travelled the long way from Cambridgeshire to be part of the ceremony. Eunice too had travelled from London and was looking forward to another discussion with Mr Pryce-Jones who had taken the service when she had last attended the church. She had already discovered that he was inclined towards high church, but he would aim to bring his parishioners round with slow persuasion rather than brute force. And apparently, the new rector was also a bachelor.

The reception took place at Copse Farm, where Farmer Hughes, who had given away the bride in the absence of Ella's late father, excelled himself with generosity and bonhomie. It was almost as though he had planned the whole thing. John's best man was Robert Moreton, who seemed to be losing weight and looking much healthier now that his father had agreed to let him take on the management of the estate. Sir Digby came to the wedding service, but could not face the rowdiness of the reception, so returned to the manor to sit among his dogs.

The happiest of all the wedding guests were Amy and George. Mrs Owen had brought George down from Lancashire and they were staying at Ella's cottage where she would be looking after both children while

John and his bride shared a brief honeymoon in Llandudno. When they returned, Ella would be moving into the schoolhouse. She had promised to assist at the school with the needlework, which unsurprisingly had not been praised by the inspector, and she would be helping the new young assistant who had taken Miss Beale's place.

The least happy wedding guest was probably Mrs Bywater. She had been much affected by the death of Harriet Owen; never imaging such a horrific event could ever happen in her own quiet village. And there had been the shock of discovering that the rector, her employer and spiritual leader, had been a lascivious man and violent murderer. There was also the shock of discovering that Harriet, who seemed so young and innocent, had not only concealed a child, but had also conducted a physical relationship with Robert Moreton. That someone she had so loved and respected should have deceived her in that way, was the most shocking thing of all.

Mrs B felt that she would no longer be needed or wanted by anyone, and her future seemed empty. Her help would no longer be required at the schoolhouse and both her daughters had left home, the eldest to marry and live far away in Birmingham, the youngest to go into service on the other side of Shrewsbury. She was pleased that John had solved the mystery of Harriet's death, but even here, she felt that she had been forgotten. Mr Noble had said they were in it together, but in the end, John had gone ahead with his investigations without keeping her informed. Mrs Bywater felt so low about everything that she had almost decided to give the wedding a miss, but on the evening before she had a visitor who changed her mind.

At first Mrs B did not recognise the little woman who had knocked on her door, although there was something familiar about her face, especially the eyes.

'Are you Mrs B?' the woman asked, in a strange accent, then added, 'Of course you are. My daughter described you so well.'

Mrs Bywater was confused for a moment, then smiled. Suddenly, and totally out of character, they embraced one another as their tears flowed.

'I wanted to meet you when you were here before, but John said it would spoil his plans to catch the murderer.'

'Aye, so this time I've come as soon as I could.'

'How is the little boy? George, isn't it?'

'He's grand. Happy to be back here in Hope, I can tell you. And with his beloved Amy again.'

'Does he look like Harriet?'

'Oh, yes. The very spit. Anyways, you'll meet him tomorrow. At the wedding.'

'Well, I...'

'John thinks the world of you, you know. And Ella too. In fact, they were wondering... No, it don't seem fair...'

'What isn't fair?'

'You've your own life to lead now. And anyway, it's up to them to ask.'

'To ask what?'

'You see, young Ella wants to educate herself, with John's help, and become a teacher too. She got the taste for it, after helping Miss Beale while John were resting his leg. They were hoping p'haps that you might still help a bit in the house, especially since there's like to be an increase in the family one of these days and…'

'I'd be delighted. You can tell them that. Nothing would please me more.'

FORTY-SEVEN

John fixed the pony's reins to the branch of a tree that had managed to survive the bitter winter winds, helped Ella down from the trap and held her in his arms. He took something from the trap and led her away from the road across the soft dry turf.

Ella hesitated for a moment. 'John... Are you sure?'

John held her at arm's length and studied her from top to toe. Her thick golden hair, which had been pinned up so carefully into an elaborate knot for the ceremony, was beginning to break out into its natural glory again. Her fair skin was still flushed with the excitement of the day, and her figure filled her dress to perfection, especially where her breasts rose and fell with anticipation. Yes, John was quite sure.

They walked together along the edge of the hill, looking back into the valley where so much had happened since John returned to Hope Underhill last September. There among the trees far below stood the tower of St Mary Magdalene and just discernible next to it the little bell tower of the school. Closer to them, but hidden by the overhang of the steep hill, was the cottage where they had first met on that lovely autumn evening. John felt his eyes drawn, unwillingly, towards Squire's Copse and to the little field beside it where that patch of barley had now been ploughed in and a veil of new growth softened the turned soil.

John's gaze rose towards the jagged ridge across the valley and he felt a slight twinge in his leg as he remembered that terrible night on Devil's Peak. He wondered how he could have misjudged Robert Moreton so badly, and what would have happened if Robert had not come back to help him out of that mine shaft.

John led Ella on again until they saw the place where the gipsy encampment had been. Old Hepzibah's stories seemed quite incredible now that the sun shone from a cloudless June sky.

At last John reached the place he had been making for, where a circle of gorse bushes almost surrounded a small glade of the mossy turf. Here he shook out the thick rug he had been carrying and laid it on the ground. He sat down and invited Ella to join him. She stood, looking down at him for a moment and said in that familiar teasing tone, 'What can you have in your mind, Mr Noble?'

'Our train doesn't leave for another hour and a half, so I thought we might have a short lesson on natural history, Mrs Noble.'

'And am I to be your only pupil today, sir?' said Ella as she sat down beside him.

'One at a time is quite enough,' he said, smiling.

Ella lay beside him on the rug and rested her head on his chest. One by one, he picked out the pins from her hair until it fell down to her shoulders. John pushed it aside and gently held her head in his hands. He looked into Ella's eyes and pressed his lips to hers. With their lips still joined he slowly moved round until Ella's body lay beneath him. He loosened his breeches and lifted her skirts. She hesitated for just a moment, before welcoming him inside her. It was the simple, honest union of man and wife.

But they were disturbed by a rustling in the surrounding gorse. John rapidly withdrew, closed his breeches and pulled down Ella's skirts. They were pink from their exertions and from the embarrassment of being discovered making love. The rustling increased and they sat up, side by side. How long had the intruder been watching they wondered? Then, through the gorse, appeared the head of a pony, their pony, which must have broken free and followed them, pulling the trap behind it. Ella burst into laughter, soon accompanied by John. She got up, straightened her skirts, went across to the pony and stroked its nose, while John folded the rug and found the reins.

As they crossed the hill on their way to Churchtown station Ella tried to make some order out of her hair, but soon gave up and simply tied it back with a ribbon like a schoolgirl.

Just as they began their descent into the next valley, they caught up with the familiar figure of Sergeant

292

Oakes making his way back from the wedding reception to take up his official duties. He gladly accepted a lift for the remainder of the journey and squeezed onto the seat beside Ella.

Oakes had married the previous January and there was already a little acorn on the way. Ella asked, 'How is Mrs Oakes?'

'Oh, she's grand. Gets mighty sick in the mornings and damned tired by th'evenings. But that's all to be expected so I'm told.' His words were rather slurred and it seemed at times as if he might tumble from the trap. Then he smiled and said, 'By, that Farmer Hughes dunna 'alf make a bloody good cider. Oops! Sorry about the language, my dear.' Suddenly, his brain broke through the fog of drink and he asked, 'How come you left the 'ception afore me, but then you comes along after me?'

Ella and John smiled at one another and he felt her arm slip round his waist and hold him tightly. John paused for a moment, then leaned across to explain.

'We decided to take a little stroll. The weather being so good and the train not due for a while.'

The policeman thought about this for a while, then continued in a serious tone. 'Ah, there ain't nuthin' like a good walk for clearin' the 'ead.' Then Oakes chuckled. 'S'long as you dunna go findin' no bodies in no barley field.'

John shuddered for a moment at the memory of that poor girl's dead body lying among the barley stalks, then joined Ella and Oakes in laughing at his grim joke, so that the trap began to shake as it rolled on down the hill.

THE END